The Return of Odysseus

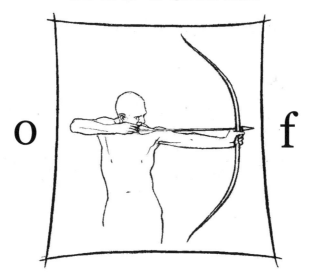

Michael Walker

SCORPION PRESS

The Return of Odysseus
By Michael Walker

Cover design © by H.P. Steadman

Scorpion Press

All material © 2015.

Email: scorpionpress@yandex.com

ISBN 978-1515340393

Contents

Cast   1

Prologue: A courtyard in the palace of Ithaca   3

Act One Scene One   11

Act One Scene Two   55

Act Two Scene One   79

Act Two Scene Two   102

Act Three Scene One   140

Act Three Scene Two   166

To Di Macnab.

Without whom this play would probably not have been written.

CAST

In order of appearance

TELEMACHUS Son of Odysseus
AGELAUS A suitor
AMPHIMEDON A suitor
ANTINOUS Leader of the suitors
CTESSIPUS A suitor
EURYMACHUS A suitor
PHEMIUS A singer
DEMOPTOLEMOS A suitor
PEISANDER A suitor
AMPHINOMUS A suitor
POLYBOS A suitor
MENTES A merchant
ODYSSEUS King of Ithaca
CALYPSO A divine spirit
AEGYPTIUS President of the Assembly
 of Ithaca
HALITHERSES A member of the
 Assembly of Ithaca
MENTOR A member of the
 Assembly of Ithaca
YOUTH A divine spirit
IRUS A beggar
PENELOPE Queen of Ithaca

Also servants

SCENE

Here and there

TIME

Now and then

Prologue: A courtyard in the palace of Ithaca.
(Telemachus is alone)

TELEMACHUS: "Welcome to my father's house. Won't you please come in?" "Sit and eat". "Sit and drink." I play the host where I have no power to decide and I smile and smile and hate myself as a coward and a hypocrite. But what else can I do? You all know the story? My father left us for a war that would never end, a war like some affliction, an ongoing sickness when, you might say to yourself, will it ever end? I am talking of that bitter and fatal siege of Ilios.

I am Telemachus, son of the king of Ithaca, the cunning Odysseus, who sailed with Agamemnon to impious Ilios. Hellas could not decide the fight in open war. It was finally my father's idea to build a huge hollow horse.

But Ilios was befriended by the sea, by the great force of the sea. Poseidon persecuted my father and they say my father has drowned. He left us nineteen years ago. Men want my mother now. They will marry her and dispossess me. I have lost all courage to oppose

them. She still waits and hopes for
some kind of wonder. They do not
hurry her because they have time
to wait and while they wait, they
despoil the island and our entire
commonwealth. More and more of
them in the most beautiful house
on this our island, this our Ithaca,
my Ithacan homeland. Welcome,
welcome, welcome.

My Ithaca, your Ithaca, whose
Ithaca? There are too many. The
island is full but they continue.
There are not only Ithacans, but
from other places too, places from
beyond Hellas even, places whose
names I hardly know.

They even sleep now in the palace
of my father and my father's father
and if they saw me they would look
at me and shake their heads that
at the end the race should taper to
such a point of enfeeblement, such
an unwillingness, such an unnatural
reluctance to stand and fight.

This is my father's palace, his palace,
but an echo, the echo of the absence
of the King. You surely know the
story. In the meantime they come
here, those we call the suitors. They
use the rooms I should inherit for
their debaucheries. We have two
dining halls, one for family meals
and one for official banquets. They

use both, all the time. Even at
night I can hear them drinking and
singing and laughing. One meal is
hardly over before our servants are
preparing for the next. Below the
flagstones in the great hall there are
granaries and parlours full of figs,
dried meat, wine and oil.
I thought I had saved those from
their greed, kept them concealed,
hoping that my father. . .hoping. . .
but Melanthius the goatherd, for
a gratuity, he showed them where
everything was stored and he let
them find the keys which in a
careless moment I had left lying
where he could find them. Each day
a servant has to go down and drag
up a new cask or barrel.
In the past they had pretexts,
"we are celebrating in honour
of Poseidon," they would say,
and I would wonder if they were
mockingly implying that my father
had had his last reckoning with that
very God, a God who haunts him
for some act of defiance.
Oh, I do not know the details but
I know their legends about him,
about my father I mean.
"In honour of the Queen of Love,"
they would say, and again I would
wonder if there was irony in their
choice of pretext. After all, they

claim all of them to love my mother.
I do not have to ask myself such
questions any longer. They have
abandoned pretexts. They merely
eat and drink and wait.

"We only claim our rights," they
say, their rights under our, "our",
republican law.

I am told my father was a tyrant and
that he oppressed the people and
I must adapt to better times and I
must renounce him, my father, my
own father, renounce him and soon
denounce him too.

Besides, they say, he is dead, sunk
they say, under the waves. Poseidon
has seen to it. Poseidon is terrible.
And I ask myself, surely they are
right. If my father were still living,
surely he would be here in Ithaca,
returned and vengeful, here on
Ithacan soil to stake his claim to his
very kingdom and rediscover the
homeland, his dear wife.

"See," they say, "be reasonable
Telemachus, be reasonable. Your
father is dead. You cannot defy
Time, the destroyer."

"He is dead," they say, he is dead,
dead and my mother must chose
her and Ithaca's future from among
the living. And my mother stays
them, still holds them back. She
seldom leaves her rooms now. I

think even she is tiring. Will he ever come back? She holds them back with a delay, with the preparation of death, with the weaving of a shroud. "I shall only marry," she tells them, "when the shroud is finally completed", my grandfather's shroud.

I have lost my status. Who calls me Prince now? I have lost my authority. If I say "do this" I am smiled at, condescended to and finally ignored.

Who do the suitors listen to? They listen to Antinous, the most confident of their arrogant tribe. I have lost my birthright; the Republic officially condemns my father as a tyrant and I am tainted as his son. I have lost my sense of honour. It would be better to put an end to this than continue in this humiliation. Perhaps all that remains is some vague call of conscience, else why could I even talk in this way to myself?

My mother reproaches me, not with words. She seldom speaks now. She reproaches me with her faith. She will not answer if someone says to her "widow"; she does not hear them. She insists we must wait. Wait, wait. It is nineteen years, nineteen years; mother, it is nineteen years. We would have heard.

Of course there have been false reports. We have heard them. They sharpen the agony, the false reports from those who help to earn easy money. But can we be sure that all the reports are false?

I do not remember my father well. I was four years old when he left for the war. I held my mother's hand. He did not turn round once. He did not wave after he had boarded the ship. He was standing at the prow of the leading ship and his cloak cast its shadow over Poseidon's Empire. The war lasted too long, much longer than we had been told. We had been promised it would be easy. It would be an easy victory.

Even the beginning had been ominous. The dispute over a sacrifice. A princess threatened with death to make the Gods favourable to the war and its outcome. All that for a woman hardly anyone had seen or spoken to! How easily wars begin, how long before there is peace and longer still or never till the memory of a war itself fades. My father was not here to see me growing. That is a consolation. He would have been disappointed. I am not a fighter. I cannot hold a sword well, and I am afraid, afraid, afraid, afraid even of my shadow, afraid especially of my shadow.

After years of waiting and rumours even of defeat, we heard rumours brought to us with increasing certainty, of a victory, of the total destruction of Ilios. Ships returned with definite affirmation.

"And all thanks to Odysseus!" they declared. The proud city had fallen. It was thanks to my father, my father with his renowned cunning tricked them to let in our men themselves, into the heart of their city. I told you: they built a horse, full of picked fighters. My father restored the honour of Menelaus, the husband whose wife impious Ilios had kidnapped.

Yes, he saved the honour of Menelaus, but what of his own honour? Father, if I am to blame as a weakling, what can I say of you, you who all this time have left me and my mother to fend alone; you have been too long away? Too long! Was it for this shame that he fought? To redeem a shame, he has created a greater shame! While he fought for Menelaus and the honour of Hellas, his own home was robbed and pillaged. When the war's end was confirmed, and

others returned and he did not and
nobody could say what had become
of him, then the suitors arrived in
increasing numbers, demanding
that my mother marry again, for the
good of the state, they said.
"She must marry one of us and
until then we are here to enjoy
everything Ithaca and the palace
can offer us," their very words. The
serving women go down to them
on bended knee and serve them to
satisfy their carnal itch while they
await my mother's decision.
And I call myself the son of
Odysseus, I call myself that when he
challenged Hector and the army of
Ilios while I linger and do nothing
about the inebriates and playboys
shaming me and my birthright.
I tell myself, hope remains, hope
still glimmers, the hope that they
never found his body, but what
hope is that? His body could be
anywhere but on that hope. I. . .
I. . . trust that the Gods will soon
bring a sign from him, a sign of
his return. It has been so long.
Nineteen years, father, nineteen
years, too long! Too long! Too long!
Gods, give me a sign. I need a sign.

Act One Scene One

A courtyard in the palace of Ithaca

(Enter Agelaus and Amphimedon, a new suitor)

AMPHIMEDON: It is better than I expected.

AGELAUS: What did you expect, Amphimedon?

AMPHIMEDON: Nothing so opulent. It was well worth my journey, but I expected it would be warmer. Why don't they light the fires? It is still cold at this time of year.

AGELAUS: The servants are kept busy clearing the latrines, preparing the tables, cooking the dinners. Anyway, the wine will warm you. There is nothing to compare to good Ithacan wine. There are some who say that we are only here for the food and drink.

AMPHIMEDON: I can think of better reasons to be here than the wine, Agelaus.

AGELAUS: There is much to criticise in Ithaca but the wine is good and the boy keeps a good table.

AMPHIMEDON: It is very quiet. I expected some sort of a reception. Where are they all?

AGELAUS: Eating. Carousing. Having a good time.

AMPHIMEDON: Having a good time?

AGELAUS: Having a good time. Having a good time. What is wrong with having a good time? What else do you expect people want to do in life?

AMPHIMEDON: And Telemachus?

AGELAUS: What of Telemachus?

AMPHIMEDON: Is he having a good time?

AGELAUS: It is not easy for him, I grant you. His own mother after all, is the prize, to put it very crudely. Telemachus behaves correctly. He does his duty as a host. He serves the customs. That is the least he can do of course. No Ithacan refuses hospitality to a compatriot. And he appears well-disposed. I mean he seems friendly enough.

AMPHIMEDON: Only seems?

AGELAUS: I won't deny that there are problems, nothing serious, personal frictions. He sometimes listens to his father's old cronies. There is always someone or other causing trouble. The old followers of the late king sometimes try to cause trouble. Some of them are quite prejudiced. Everything is taking too long, moving far too slowly, in my opinion.

AMPHIMEDON: Prejudice? In Ithaca?

AGELAUS: Hidden prejudice. Cowardly prejudice.

AMPHIMEDON: Against, against..?

AGELAUS: People like you and me.

AMPHIMEDON: I was born on this island and I have never noticed prejudice.

AGELAUS: You were born into a wealthy family. Where there is money, people hide their feelings better. Nothing is so raw. People do not expose themselves to contempt.

AMPHIMEDON: I do not follow you.

AGELAUS: Telemachus is a hypocrite. When he says "welcome" do not believe him. He says "welcome" because he is compelled. It is custom, he is a coward. He looks at the people around him and thinks to himself, so must I comport myself; but if you could see into his soul like a God,

then you would see his prejudice
and a seething contempt for us
awaiting its opportunity. Do not
believe his smiles, his laughs, his
endearments. Behind our backs he
smirks and sneers. He considers us
inferior. He spreads rumours, or at
the very least he does nothing to
prevent them.
His sympathisers say worse about
us, in the Assembly, using the
protection of privilege.

AMPHIMEDON: These things take time to change but
they will.

AGELAUS: Be prepared in him for what I call
the temptation to authority. He is, all
said and done, the son of a pirate, a
brigand, a freebooter, the man who
brought terror to the Aegean seas.
He is in his heart an oligarch.

AMPHIMEDON: And there are still those who speak
of his life and a return, the King's. . .
I mean, the pirate's.

AGELAUS: Those who believe that the tyrant
was in the right when he pillaged are
those who whisper now he may still
return. It is not reason but wishful
thinking which makes them say so.
It is what they want to believe and so
they say they believe it. They are the

people who hate and fear the word
"inevitable", who believe the course
of time can be changed at will.

AMPHIMEDON: The same people, no doubt, who
want to eject us, send us back, as
they charmingly term it.

AGELAUS: We shall never leave. We are here to
stay.

AMPHIMEDON: I know that!

AGELAUS: Not for her sake.

AMPHIMEDON: For the wine?

AGELAUS: Neither for that queen nor for any
wine, however good.

AMPHIMEDON: I have come here for the wine,
among other things; I have heard
good things about the palace wine.

AGELAUS: If you are motivated by wine
and general relaxation, then you are
like most of them, thoroughly
superficial.

AMPHIMEDON: What do you mean?

AGELAUS: I tell you, there is a political issue
to be decided here. The man who
wins Penelope will rule Ithaca. Some

suitors are only here to have a good time.

AMPHIMEDON: And you? What are you here for?

AGELAUS: I am here out of principle.

AMPHIMEDON: Principle!

AGELAUS: Yes, principle. Not something you hear too often nowadays, is it? Principle, I mean. I am not here for myself; I am here to see that the best is done for the country.
(To Amphimedon) Do you think that's funny?

AMPHIMEDON: Not exactly funny, but a little hard to believe.

AGELAUS: Why hard to believe?

AMPHIMEDON: I just can't see what principle is involved here. Rights maybe, but not principles. We are suitors to the widow, that's all.

AGELAUS: That's all? That's all? "All" is the future of this country.

AMPHIMEDON: Well yes, I suppose so.

AGELAUS: The destiny of a nation.

AMPHIMEDON: Oh I understand that. Don't think for a moment I am not in earnest.

AGELAUS: In earnest? In earnest about what?

AMPHIMEDON: Marrying the widow.

AGELAUS: And why?

AMPHIMEDON: Why?

AGELAUS: Yes why? Why? What is your interest in her?

AMPHIMEDON: Well. . .

AGELAUS: Money?

AMPHIMEDON: Money. Who dislikes money?

AGELAUS: And power?

AMPHIMEDON: Of course, power too.

AGELAUS: Power for what?

AMPHIMEDON: Power to rule and decide.

AGELAUS: Democratically, to rule democratically?

AMPHIMEDON: Well you don't expect me to say that I wish for the restoration of tyranny here. Nobody wants that. I am not an oligarch.

AGELAUS: Not one of us wants tyranny? You are wrong. You are young and naive.

AMPHIMEDON: There are a few reactionaries who dream of a long lost past.

AGELAUS: But we must be vigilant. The price of freedom is eternal vigilance! The new king must be one who believes in the democratic right to a voice. No man has the right to another's property except through law and barter. The days of pillage will be ended for ever. So my question: what will you do with your power if you become the lucky choice? This choice is not a personal choice, it is not or not only an economic one. It is deeply political. No one who is not democratic, not so to speak, democratic to their fingertips, should be considered for the honour.

AMPHIMEDON: Oh yes, democracy is important.

AGELAUS: Not just important, supremely important. Government for and by the people. That is the end of history my friend. That or damnation.

(Enter Telemachus)

TELEMACHUS: Agelaus, I see you have brought a new guest here.

AGELAUS: Yes. May I introduce a new hopeful, Amphimedon. He has come here in the hope that he will be the fortunate man to be chosen one day by your royal mother.

TELEMACHUS: So I imagine, so I imagine. Welcome. You will find that this is more than a house.

AGELAUS: A palace, not a house. There are scores of rooms. Below the flags in the great hall are granaries and store rooms where wine is stored, salted meat, spices, figs, honey, milk and jars of oil.

AMPHIMEDON: Melanthius has kindly showed me everything.

TELEMACHUS: Only one room is out of bounds. Have you told him Agelaus?

AMPHIMEDON: Being?

AGELAUS: The bed chamber of . . .

AMPHIMEDON: Of course, of course. Until the day when, when, when everything is resolved . . .

AGELAUS: Are you coming with us, Telemachus?

TELEMACHUS:	Coming with you? Where to?
AGELAUS:	The feast of course, the celebrations.
AMPHIMEDON:	The feast today in honour of the Queen of Love.
AGELAUS:	That is why Amphimedon came on this day.
AMPHIMEDON:	One could say that all days here are days in her honour.
AGELAUS:	Today is special, Telemachus. We are hoping that the Queen of Love will enter your mother's heart and direct her eyes.
AMPHIMEDON:	And move her..
AGELAUS:	Move her to a choice. We are counting on it.
TELEMACHUS:	Then go and enjoy yourselves.
AGELAUS:	You will not come?
TELEMACHUS:	Just go. I'm, fine. Please just go.
AGELAUS:	We shall see you later.

(They bow to Telemachus and exeunt).

TELEMACHUS:	Antinous! No one there? Antinous!

(Enter Antinous)

ANTINOUS: I am here. I am always here.

TELEMACHUS: Another.

ANTINOUS: Another?

TELEMACHUS: Suitor of course.

ANTINOUS: So, what of it? One more or less,
              what is the difference? I never said
              there would be no more suitors at
              all, I only said that numbers of new
              applicants would continue to fall.

TELEMACHUS: You promised that I would not have
              to worry about new suitors.

ANTINOUS: Exactly. I said there was no need to
              worry about new suitors and there is
              indeed no need.
              This latest one is some unimportant
              friend of Agelaus.
              I don't wish to upset Agelaus and
              we can afford to let him have the
              occasional friend. One suitor more
              or less will not matter. We can afford
              to bend the rules.

TELEMACHUS: How many more. Can you give at
              least a figure? Two, three, ten?

ANTINOUS: Very well. If this is so important to
              you, I can arrange to ensure that this
              was the last new suitor.

TELEMACHUS: Oh what does it matter, you are right, it makes no difference if one more comes or two or three.

ANTINOUS: I promise you, there will be no more.

TELEMACHUS: There are enough as it is, with their appetites, to ruin this estate.

ANTINOUS: We are here for one thing only, and that one thing is not to ruin your estate.

TELEMACHUS: So you keep telling me, but by Republican law, I stand to lose the entire estate.

ANTINOUS: It is only justice.

TELEMACHUS: Do you call it justice when you claim that all men are equal?

ANTINOUS: And women too. I say this: it is just and legal that suitors are here and that you acknowledge your father's wrongs committed against the people.

TELEMACHUS: They will believe you now. You have taken away my authority. It is you they obey.

ANTINOUS: Would you rather they obeyed no man? Would you rather have anarchy in Ithaca?

TELEMACHUS: I had rather that you listened, that you did what we wish; all of you just, leave!

ANTINOUS: The Republic, the entire Assembly, condemned your father by due process of law.

TELEMACHUS: The Republic makes the law today, not kings.

ANTINOUS: I never favoured it. If she chooses me, there will be a monarchy again.

TELEMACHUS: My father...

ANTINOUS: Your father, your father! He paid for his crimes.

TELEMACHUS: Was fighting in the name of Ithaca a crime?

ANTINOUS: He conquered by guile, subterfuge and cruelty.

TELEMACHUS: He ended the war.

ANTINOUS: By guile.

TELEMACHUS: If it were not for him, our armies might still be festering there in Ilios, those accursed camps before the walls.

ANTINOUS: If it were not for your father and his kind, the war might never have begun.

TELEMACHUS: Then Ilios would still be standing.

ANTINOUS: Where?

TELEMACHUS: Troy.

ANTINOUS: And many mother's sons be still alive, yes.

TELEMACHUS: Ilios, Troy, would have destroyed us all.

ANTINOUS: Perhaps, perhaps not. These are old quarrels.

TELEMACHUS: No peace came from there.

ANTINOUS: If you insist, no peace came from Troy. Argue this among your friends. History is history. The present is what concerns me.

TELEMACHUS: My father ended the war and recovered the honour of Menelaus.

ANTINOUS: Honour is a slogan, a shibboleth. It has no tangible value.

TELEMACHUS: But those who criticise my father say the stratagem of the wooden horse was dishonourable.
Dishonourable. That's the very word they use.

ANTINOUS: It is not a word that I use.

TELEMACHUS: Nor I, the word chokes me.

ANTINOUS: I prefer to talk of conscience. That is the word people prefer to use today.

TELEMACHUS: Conscience, honour, they say to me, "Telemachus you are weak, as weak as water".

ANTINOUS: And what is your weakness?

TELEMACHUS: That I am a coward, a coward through and through, all the time, I slink away from any and every challenge.

ANTINOUS: Well many of us are. Even your mother, perhaps especially your mother. She is called the "timorous widow" you know. Did you know that?

TELEMACHUS: She is not a widow!

ANTINOUS: You mean she is timorous? Well she is both. I find the nickname apt. She is a widow. He will not return, Telemachus.
Your father will not return. Accept it. Just accept it. Try, try to accept reality. This change is inevitable. Accept the inevitable and dream in private. We can indulge your dreams.

TELEMACHUS: How can you possibly be so sure he will not return? And why are you afraid?

ANTINOUS: Afraid? What should I be afraid of?

TELEMACHUS: You are afraid of a possible return. You are, you are afraid. I know you are afraid. I smell it. I can smell your fear, in all of you.

ANTINOUS: You do not understand what is happening in Ithaca. Kings will no longer dictate to us. Those days are over my friend, and good riddance. Do you even remember him, this father whom you feel dishonoured? You are too young.

TELEMACHUS: It is true that he left us for the war when I was only three. But I remember holding my mother's hand and watching from the harbour. He did not turn round once. I remember that. I remember hoping that he would turn round and wave. He was standing at the prow of the leading ship. His cloak seemed to cast a shadow over the wine dark surface of Poseidon's Empire.

ANTINOUS: The wine dark surface of Poseidon's Empire! Quite the poet! Now there is a future for you, as a poet.

TELEMACHUS: Later we heard stories and rumours
of the war and the long, the
unexpectedly long siege.

ANTINOUS: Yes, everyone had expected the war
to finish in weeks.

TELEMACHUS: All my childhood was marked by
reports from the war, some
favourable, some worrying.

ANTINOUS: The promises of early and easy
victory were bluster and propaganda.

TELEMACHUS: Then came reports of a great victory.
We could not be sure at first, but
it was confirmed and confirmed
again.
The first ships returned. Troy had
been destroyed, razed to the ground.
Someone escaped with his father.

ANTINOUS: Aeneas.

TELEMACHUS: Swearing revenge on Greece, on us
all.

ANTINOUS: No one heard any news from him
again.

TELEMACHUS: My father, they said, was returning
too, returning too, and we waited.
We are still waiting.

ANTINOUS: Waiting and waiting. Probably some people, some relatives who cannot face the inevitable are waiting for Aeneas too, with the same inevitable result.

TELEMACHUS: The ships of the heroes were one day out of eyesight and the weaklings and parasites came out to feed on my father's estate.

(Enter Ctessipus)

CTESSIPUS: Antinous, I am pleased to see you looking so fit after last night's extravagance. I myself have not properly recovered.

ANTINOUS: Ctessipus! I hope you have recovered sufficiently to enjoy the revels planned for tonight.

CTESSIPUS: No, no. It is a celebration for younger people. What have I to do with the Queen of Love?

ANTINOUS: Never say die, my friend! Never say die! It is getting late and you remind me. . .
Gentlemen, I must leave. I am wanted for the preparations.

(Exit Antinous)

CTESSIPUS: Marvellous man, great prince, leader of men. Antinous is the one. Antinous is the one.

TELEMACHUS: If he is the one, what makes you linger here?

CTESSIPUS: I like it here. I sleep here. I eat here. I....I...vote here.

TELEMACHUS: The palace belongs to me. It is my birthright.

CTESSIPUS: So sad. You cannot keep off one subject all day long. You are obsessed. But I can understand you. The strain is telling on all of us. This has all gone on too long. You are young and angry and impetuous.
We are all getting impatient. We are all asking ourselves: when will she marry? When will she make the announcement?

TELEMACHUS: When she has finished the shroud, she said when she has finished the shroud.

CTESSIPUS: The shroud, oh yes, the shroud. If she doesn't hurry it will be my shroud. I am curious. I am so curious to know how things will go.

TELEMACHUS: Men will not remember you.

CTESSIPUS: Nor women. And you remember your father, as an ideal perhaps, an example to follow. That's all right. It is natural in fact.

Others remember him and would rather forget. The past is a nightmare for many, a nightmare of exploitation and greed.

You are just one man who cannot accept the way the world has turned. Old men like Mentor, I can expect to be a little nostalgic, for creating a past which is more glorious and more gentle than the real past. They are too old to change, but you are young and you are wasting your time and energy in hoping for the return of what has been irretrievably and inevitably lost. The new world is yours for the having and you persist in looking back and hoping for messages from the dead. Leave the dead alone Telemachus. They are dead and have nothing to say to the living.

TELEMACHUS: It is your world, the change is to your world.

CTESSIPUS: I am an old man. I am many years older than you. I have seen many changes in the world. I like some of them. I do not like others. But strangely I can better understand

and live in the new order than you can. Telemachus, the time is coming when you will have to accommodate yourself to one of us. Your mother cannot delay indefinitely. Antinous will not be patient indefinitely.

TELEMACHUS: I told you, she will not decide until..

CTESSIPUS: She has finished that shroud, that wretched shroud, that ominous shroud. I know what she said. Your mother's delays are over, Telemachus, over.

TELEMACHUS: The shroud, the shroud! Not before the shroud is finished. Not before the shroud is finished. You all promised. Do you break oaths now? Do you laugh at the gods? Have we come this far?

CTESSIPUS: Is that what prevents you joining us in persuading her to decide? Is that all? This shroud? Then let me tell you now, although I had wanted to conceal this for a while; well never mind, you will learn soon enough, you can learn now. It concerns your mother. For all the suitors, hopeful news.

TELEMACHUS: I will not believe it! She has not weakened!

CTESSIPUS: Weakening you call it? What a foolish expression! Realism, not weakening. Realism! Realism! It is impossible to change anything now. No, no. She is showing no sign of what you call weakening. She must be called to account.

TELEMACHUS: What are you trying to tell me, then? What is your news? Are you claiming she has broken some regulation?

CTESSIPUS: If it were only that, there would be gallant suitors for her hand who would excuse her. No, it is worse than that, far worse. She is practising deceit on all of us, on you too I expect because I do not think you know either.

TELEMACHUS: Know what?

CTESSIPUS: Eurymachus thinks that you know all about it but I disagree. I think she has fooled you as well. This is embarrassing.

TELEMACHUS: Tell me. Stop talking in riddles!

CTESSIPUS: I believe you have no idea. It concerns the shroud. The shroud, the shroud for Laertes, may his soul rest in peace.

TELEMACHUS: The shroud for Laertes, the shroud, and?

CTESSIPUS: She promised to choose her husband when she had completed that shroud.

TELEMACHUS: I know that and Antinous agreed.

CTESSIPUS: Yes. Antinous, naïve, honest, gentle man agreed. Eurymachus was opposed from the beginning. Laertes' body is preserved in oils, which is a very good thing. Do you know how long the Queen has been working on Laertes' shroud?

TELEMACHUS: A while.

CTESSIPUS: A while, you call it. There are whiles and whiles, my friend. The Queen's while is a long while. Tomorrow it will have been one year two months and three weeks and five days. It is a long while to make a winding sheet.

TELEMACHUS: I would not know. I am not an expert.

CTESSIPUS: You know it is a long while, a very long while.

TELEMACHUS: If you say so.

CTESSIPUS: You know it is a long time! I had
              thought for some time that there
              will be little of a corpse of Laertes to
              wind up at the rate she is winding
              this shroud.

TELEMACHUS: Is old Laertes dead then?

CTESSIPUS: Dead or not dead, that isn't relevant.
              She was told he had died.
              I had been thinking for a long time
              that it was convenient, this slow
              dying of Laertes, this winding sheet.
              I thought, does she remember old
              Laertes as a Titan, that she needs a
              massive sheet?" I made allowances
              for the care I would expect her to
              take, of course, and the leisurely
              pace she might be tempted to take,
              that too, the intricate patterns, the
              fine material.
              Perhaps sometimes I thought she
              had to undo some part of her work.
              Then it occurred to me she might be
              often tempted to undo some of her
              work. I spoke to Melanthius about
              it, and he understood me and we
              agreed that we should check to
              ensure that my doubts were quite
              unfounded. We took the liberty to
              observe her at work.

TELEMACHUS: You spied! You spied on my mother!

CTESSIPUS: You use very vulgar expressions. Whether you call it spying or what you want to call it, we discovered that my fears were not groundless. It was exactly as I suggested to Melanthius.

TELEMACHUS: Spies, in her own house!

CTESSIPUS: Your father was aggressive like you and see where that brought him.

TELEMACHUS: Where did it bring him?

CTESSIPUS: Into the salt-smelling and dark embrace of Poseidon.

TELEMACHUS: And you are pleased. You all hated him when he was alive but you never had the courage then, any of you.

CTESSIPUS: So uncouth.

TELEMACHUS: You have the audacity to tell me you were spying and I just stand there. I should wring your neck.

CTESSIPUS: Control yourself man! Are you drunk?

TELEMACHUS: You spied!

(Enter Eurymachus)

EURYMACHUS: Telemachus, you know now? So Ctessipus has croaked. Yes, he spied through a crack in the door to the royal bedchamber.

TELEMACHUS: Eurymachus, what do you know of all this?

EURYMACHUS: I just heard a reference to the Queen, the Gods bless her, and I guessed at once that Ctessipus had talked too much.

TELEMACHUS: (*To Ctessipus*) What does he mean?

CTESSIPUS: I had mentioned that Penelope. . .

EURYMACHUS: Queen Penelope, please.

CTESSIPUS: That Queen Penelope had been deceiving us all. She hasn't been fair.

EURYMACHUS: Crudely expressed perhaps, but essentially true, Telemachus.

CTESSIPUS: Tell him yourself then.

EURYMACHUS: What do you want me to say?

CTESSIPUS: That the shroud is a fraud. A fraud, like the Spartan military code, the honour of Menelaus and his father's religious horse. The way we won the war, call it hoax if you prefer. What's in a word?

EURYMACHUS: Telemachus, what he means is that your mother has not been honestly working on the shroud.

CTESSIPUS: The sewing of the shroud was a fraud..

TELEMACHUS: I've seen the shroud. I've seen my mother working on it. Old Laertes' shroud.

CTESSIPUS: And a very beautiful piece of work it is too, if I may so so, but she is committing sabotage.

TELEMACHUS: I do not understand.

CTESSIPUS: You are obtuse, young man.

TELEMACHUS: Just tell me what you claim she has done or is doing wrong.

EURYMACHUS: From her point of view, nothing.

CTESSIPUS: She unties it again at night.

EURYMACHUS: The shroud.

CTESSIPUS: If you want, you can watch too.

EURYMACHUS: I defended your mother's delay out of respect for custom. Now I shall be accused of diplomatic cunning, or worse. How could she, Telemachus? How could she? Betray our trust?

CTESSIPUS: She took advantage of our good faith really.

TELEMACHUS: Your good faith you call it!

CTESSIPUS: Yes, it never occurred to anyone she would use a trick like that. Now it is out, now we know. Think about it, Telemachus. *(Exit)*

TELEMACHUS: Eurymachus, is this true?

EURYMACHUS: I wish I could say that the old fool was lying, but he isn't. I saw it with my own eyes.

TELEMACHUS: Will he tell the others?

EURYMACHUS: He told me immediately he saw me. Yes, I am sure he will.

TELEMACHUS: And how do you think the others will react?

EURYMACHUS: Your mother has made them look like idiots. They will hate that. Of course, I shall object to any recriminations which may be raised in the Assembly and any attempt to restrict her movements. In the meantime, we are just going to have to ride over this calamity.

TELEMACHUS: It is not a calamity. You exaggerate, surely.

EURYMACHUS:	Have you seen Antinous angry? He will regard it as extremely serious and insulting to have wasted his time for so long, to have been made a fool of. He will say that his good faith has been exploited with the use of subterfuge. Now they will force the issue to a head.

TELEMACHUS:	Who will?

EURYMACHUS:	Agelaus and the rest. They'll force Antinous to hand the Queen an ultimatum. I don't see how Antinous could stop them.

TELEMACHUS:	Does that matter to you? It is what you want!

EURYMACHUS:	Antinous does not want that. He has enemies. If the marriage is announced without a due period of engagement, there could be objections in the Assembly. Demoptolemus will certainly protest and if Agelaus can use him, he will second the objections.

TELEMACHUS:	What could they do once my mother has announced her consent to Antinous?

EURYMACHUS:	There are a number of possible ploys. They might choose to argue that

your mother and Antinous were
conspiring against them.

TELEMACHUS: That makes no sense. If my mother
had agreed to marry Antinous, she
would have already proclaimed the
fact.

EURYMACHUS: Not necessarily. For a long time
your mother has been expecting the
return of the. . .your father.
She might arguably have reached an
agreement with Antinous that she
would marry him at a given later
date provided he agreed to support
her in her delaying tactics for a
given period. I can imagine that
when this story about the shroud
becomes common knowledge,
Agelaus will argue that those suitors
who have no hope of success have
connived with the Queen because
they enjoy living here and want to
defer a decision as long as they can.
They let her use tricks to delay a
decision and in the meantime they
enjoy the good life.
After all, they cannot expect
someone like Antinous to be so
generous to them as you are,
especially given the fact that once he
marries your mother, they will not
have the ghost of an excuse for
staying on here.

The broad and the long of it is that this scandal will force people to say publicly what they have been asking themselves for months in private, namely why is the Queen taking so very long to decide and is anyone aiding and abetting?

For his part, Demoptolemos might chose to argue that this is a plot against democracy, that Antinous wants to become a Tyrant.

He might go on to argue that agreeing on any marriage should only be made with majority consent in the Assembly.

TELEMACHUS: But that could mean that they never decide and remain for years, for ever.

EURYMACHUS: That's right. They are extremely comfortable here, all of them. She should be allowed to marry whom she pleases. It is the custom in Ithaca that a woman chooses her own husband.

TELEMACHUS: Suppose none of you pleases her, none of you ever has?

EURYMACHUS: That is impossible, as you well know. The important thing is to smooth things over now by forestalling the outburst which is sure to come. I can

do that by suggesting to Antinous
that we name a date for the naming
of the lucky man.
She will be forced in any case to
decide soon. I once heard Ctessipus
joke that he will die before she comes
to a decision.
There is something else to consider.

TELEMACHUS: Namely?

EURYMACHUS: Namely that in a few more years she
will have become too old.

TELEMACHUS: Too old?

EURYMACHUS: Telemachus please! Are you really so
obtuse? Antinous wants her to carry
his breed. Surely that is obvious,
even to you.

TELEMACHUS: I didn't, I don't think about that!

EURYMACHUS: You should, you should.
Imagine alternatively your mother
bearing the breed of Demoptolemos.

TELEMACHUS: Vile!

EURYMACHUS: If you think so, if you think so, call
it vile, vile but not impossible. After
the news of her deceit the Assembly
will be enraged. If I cannot placate
them, or at least placate Antinous,

they might be willing to counsel
some fantastic democratic proposal
from Demoptolemos, for example
making the Queen choose her
husband by having the suitors all
pick straws. That would give the less
favoured an equal chance with the
rest. Now can you see why Antinous
is anxious? Now do you understand
that her delays will not help her? On
the contrary, she is making matters
worse for herself and for everyone.
Imagine her given to Ctessipus. His
breath smells of the fish stalls in
summer, or how about Agelaus
with his rotting black teeth and his
rages, or best of all, Demoptolemos,
who, I am told, suffers from a
contagious skin disease and whose
rags cover a body alive with cankers,
carbuncles. I myself have counted
the lice in his beard and on his head.
There are so many that they remind
me of the hustle and bustle of the
summer markets.

TELEMACHUS: Stop! That's enough!

EURYMACHUS: Face reality. Change is inevitable.
He will not return. He is drowned.
It is Poseidon's revenge. He angered
Poseidon after that business with his
one eyed son. Even the Queen must
know in her heart that it is time
to accept the new order. Tell her to

43

choose and to choose Antinous. She will listen to you. You are the only person she will listen to. Tell her. And by the way, I have instructions from Antinous to prepare the draft of a new regulation which will ban all new suitors from the palace unless he is granted a special dispensation. He told me to tell you that is being done in response to a complaint which you lodged a short time ago. You see, he does listen to you, Telemachus.

TELEMACHUS: Is that not illegal?

EURYMACHUS: That is correct. Technically the Assembly must decide. But who would object? Demoptolemos? He would not dare. In fact he is already frightened. And I don't expect that young Telemachus will be running to the law courts on such an issue.

TELEMACHUS: How do I put up with this?

EURYMACHUS: Put up with what exactly?

TELEMACHUS: You, all of you, being here, being here!

EURYMACHUS: I understand, in fact you know I even sympathise. It must be harrowing at times here in the

country you were born in and
in the house where you were born to
be surrounded by strangers, no
news of your father, lost, presumed
missing let's say, and the strangers
making fun of you behind your
back, sometimes hardly behind your
back at all any more and abusing
your hospitality, wasting your good
wine, plundering the stores.
You sometimes do not hide your
indignation and practically forget
the laws of hospitality and I can well
understand that.
I have a heart you know. Some of
your claims are quite justified and it
is wrong of Antinous to have denied
them in the past; your complaint
concerning the offensive behaviour
of some of the suitors, Agelaus for
example, strikes me as being at least
partly justified.
The trouble is however, you over-
simplify and ignore the fact that
some of us are sympathetic to many
of your criticisms of the suitors.
Remember that some of us, and I am
one of them, are only here out of a
sense of duty.
We are all awaiting one decision and
when that decision is made, the
problem, if it is a problem, will have
resolved itself. It will evaporate with
one word from your mother.

TELEMACHUS: There are too many of you.

EURYMACHUS: Quite so. I am always defending
you after one of your outbursts on
those grounds.
I say to someone like Agelaus or
Ctessipus: put yourself in his shoes.
It cannot be a joy to have so many
guests in his father's house drinking
his father's wine as though it were
theirs, without a by-your-leave!
She should have pity on her son if
not on us!
By the way, did you know that
Antinous is constantly defending
her? No one dare breathe a word
of criticism if Antinous is within
hearing.
He slapped Ctessipus, just imagine,
a man twice his age at least, slapped
him and quite hard too, for making
a remark about the Queen which
Antinous considered disreopertful.
It was quite harmless too.

TELEMACHUS: What did he say?

EURYMACHUS: Oh nothing, you do not need to
know. Nothing. Telemachus, the
discovery of her subterfuge will
change the situation.
It will affect his attitude to her. He
will say, "Is this gratitude?"
His feelings will be wounded.
Antinous is proud. Speak to her,

Telemachus. This land is
leaderless.

TELEMACHUS: What can I say to her?

EURYMACHUS: Tell he it is her patriotic duty to
marry.

TELEMACHUS: I did that, yes I did that.

EURYMACHUS: Really! You never told me. How did
she react?

TELEMACHUS: She looked at me in sorrow. She said,
no, she said it was her patriotic duty
to wait, to continue to wait.

EURYMACHUS: Such stubbornness! Well, do you
think she is waiting or just delaying?

TELEMACHUS: Possibly it is all the same to her,
delaying is waiting and waiting is
delaying. And possibly she is right.

EURYMACHUS: Do not delude yourself. You will
never lead a free life if you believe
that.

TELEMACHUS: You said just now that Ithaca is
leaderless.

EURYMACHUS: Yes, leaderless.

TELEMACHUS: I thought the Republic repudiated
the leadership principle.

EURYMACHUS: Of course it does. The Republic rejects the principle of leadership, which does not mean we do not have leaders. That would be silly. In reality we of course still need leaders. Without leadership, Ithaca would sooner or later fall under the sway of anarchy, the rule of Demoptolemos and fanatics like him, who believe that all gods are equal, all men equal and women too, and slaves for all I know.

TELEMACHUS: Slaves! You are not serious!

EURYMACHUS: Demoptolemos is extravagant, so extreme that he takes every argument to its furthest possible conclusion. I have not heard him say that slaves should have political rights, but I would not be at all surprised if he did argue that. According to him and his followers, there will be no distinction, nothing between one of us and another. Of course there is method in his madness. With a body such as his, it is unsurprising that he preaches the equality of all the suitors. And your mother is helping him.

TELEMACHUS: My mother is the last person...

EURYMACHUS: To be helping him? Oh quite. I am not disputing that. Consciously she

would not dream of helping him
but the reality is different. She helps
him with her delay. He feeds on
delays and grows daily stronger with
them and I am speaking literally too,
as your cooks will be aware. The
man is a scrounger, that is the
best word to describe him, otherwise
I would call him maniac, perverter
of the common good, maggot of the
commonwealth, filthy unshaven
extremist.

Thwart your enemies, Telemachus. I
speak to you as a friend. Announce
her marriage.

TELEMACHUS: She must decide. I cannot decide in
her place.

EURYMACHUS: Your duty is to help her. She wastes
her weeks, weaving, unweaving,
gazing out to sea where all is quite
and stays quiet. Faith belongs to
dreamers. She must become a realist
and accept the inevitable. She must
assume responsibility. And if it is
faith which she needs, she should
show faith in Antinous.

TELEMACHUS: She has faith in my father.

EURYMACHUS: I expect they have finished eating
by now. Come with me to the dining
hall. We shall hear Phemius on the

harp if we go now. He plays well and
he has a lovely voice.

(Enter Phemius)

EURYMACHUS: Phemius, we are sorry to have
missed you. I was just saying to
Telemachus here that we should go
to listen to you.

PHEMIUS: They were not in the mood for
music. Antinous is angry.

EURYMACHUS: Angry?

PHEMIUS: You know why.

EURYMACHUS: But you sang today?

PHEMIUS: I sang, yes.

EURYMACHUS·   What did you sing?

PHEMIUS: The story of the horse.

EURYMACHUS: Does he like that story? It has
become a legend.

PHEMIUS: A living legend.

EURYMACHUS: Boy, it is hardly living.

PHEMIUS: Antinous feels it as a living legend.
And I sang another song from the
war.

EURYMACHUS: Another song?

PHEMIUS: Achilles and Patroclus.

TELEMACHUS: Achilles and...?

PHEMIUS: Patroclus.

TELEMACHUS: I do not know that story

PHEMIUS: That song? Achilles was in a rage. He would not fight. He remained in his tent by day and night.

EURYMACHUS: A childish and perverse story from the war. You are not missing much if you do not know it, Telemachus.

PHEMIUS: Nothing would induce him to come out. Sulky man. Man in umbrage. Until the day. Until the day.

TELEMACHUS: What day, what day?

EURYMACHUS: Perverse and childish, not manly.

TELEMACHUS: What day?

PHEMIUS: The day when Hector felled Patroclus. A day that would be doom to Ilios, the first step of doom before the horse.
Like a tree Patroclus fell, Patroclus the brave, Patroclus the beautiful.

He has killed my child, Achilles
cried! He has struck the roots!

TELEMACHUS: And then?

PHEMIUS: Arose Achilles a giant in the grief of
his people and put his armour on.
He hacked his way to Hector and
chased Hector round the walls, three
times. He struck tall Hector down.
That blood for the cause of my grief,
he cried!
See Hector the mighty is fallen. The
light of Ilios extinguished by mighty
grief. Such is the rage of lovers in
grief.

TELEMACHUS: And was that proper of Achilles?

PHEMIUS: Proper? What do you mean proper?
What has Achilles' grief to do with
proper actions?
It was necessary, properly necessary,
if you will. They were not our people,
they were not Greeks. They spoke
another tongue. No-one could
understand them.

EURYMACHUS: Fighting, fighting, fighting and
dying.
But the story is hardly proper.

PHEMIUS: Men are born for three things only,
to create, to love and to fight.

EURYMACHUS: Create, love, fight! You are too young to understand these things.

PHEMIUS: Now they are fighting among each other and do not need me.

EURYMACHUS: What about?

PHEMIUS: Ctessipus said something about the Queen, some kind of trick she had used.

EURYMACHUS: That is what I feared. Telemachus, Ctessipus would not keep quiet.

TELEMACHUS: It makes me sick to listen to them. What can I do there? What can I change?

EURYMACHUS: You must come with me and talk with them. People will say you are hiding.

TELEMACHUS: Hiding!

EURYMACHUS: Yes, hiding. You will be known as a coward.

TELEMACHUS: I often avoid their meetings. Why should they think differently of me if I avoid this one too?

EURYMACHUS: Because of Ctessipus. He has told them about the Queen and he will tell them more. He is very capable of lying. I'll stand up for you and your mother but you must be seen there with me. If you are there, it will make a good impression. People will listen.

TELEMACHUS: As you like.

EURYMACHUS: Good. I'm glad you are showing some spirit.

(Exeunt)

Act One Scene Two

The Dining Hall

All the suitors except Eurymachus are present. A banquet has just finished. The suitors are still being served. A dog can be heard baying.

ANTINOUS: And what have you to say about this, Demoptolemus? You are unusually quiet.

DEMOPTOLEMUS: I am thinking.

ANTINOUS: A welcome change. And what about you Agelaus? Have you any objections?

AGELAUS: Why should I have? Your plan is reasonable....

ANTINOUS: Ctessipus, you never miss a feast here. It is a wonder that you do not bring your rugs and come to live here permanently. The palace is something like a club for you. Today however, you have brought us more than words and appreciation of this hospitality. Will someone silence that dismal dog?

(A servant exits. Sound ceases)

AGELAUS: Pining for its master.

AMPHINOMUS: A bad omen.

ANTINOUS: If omens frighten you, Amphinomus, let me remind you that are under no obligation to remain here.

(Enter Eurymachus and Telemachus)

ANTINOUS: Eurymachus, Telemachus, welcome. You have come late to eat, but I am sure that Melanthius could organise some light supper for you both.

AGELAUS: Tell them, Antinous.

EURYMACHUS: We know, we know.

ANTINOUS: About Penelope?

EURYMACHUS: About the Queen.

ANTINOUS: Eurymachus, did you know about this already?

EURYMACHUS: I knew already, yes.

ANTINOUS: Ctessipus has told us. Had you hoped to keep it as your little secret from the rest of us? I cannot imagine that you could be so deceitful.

EURYMACHUS: It was my hope.

ANTINOUS: Why?

EURYMACHUS: This is a very delicate matter.

AGELAUS: Answer the question!

ANTINOUS: Why, Eurymachus?

EURYMACHUS: You know now anyway, that should be enough for you.

ANTINOUS: We have made a decision in your absence, not that your presence or that of young Prince Telemachus would have changed anything to a majority opinion. With one abstention, otherwise unanimously, we have agreed to issue the Queen with an ultimatum.

EURYMACHUS: I advise against that.

PEISANDER: Before you start advising anyone here what to do, I suggest you tell us why you wanted to keep this trickery a secret.

AGELAUS: And what you have been discussing with him. *(Nodding in the direction of Telemachus).*

EURYMACHUS: You realise that you will have to present your plans to the Assembly for approval?

ANTINOUS: I know the law as well as anyone in this country, Eurymachus.

AGELAUS: So? What of it? Will you try to stop us?

AMPHINOMUS: He can't!

EURYMACHUS: One moment, please. Have you considered the shame, humility and scandal? People will laugh at you. They will say, "the clever Antinous was fooled by a woman". Is that what you want?

AGELAUS: She abused our trust! It is her fault and her fault alone!

EURYMACHUS: Never mind the fault.

CTESSIPUS: If there had been decent servants, we should have learned of this before.

ANTINOUS: Ctessipus, that's hardly relevant now. You were saying, Eurymachus.

EURYMACHUS: People will see this differently.

AMPHINEMON: What voice will be raised against us in the Assembly, apart from Mentor's voice?

AGELAUS: And who pays attention to that old reactionary?

EURYMACHUS: I am not talking about the Assembly, Agelaus.

AGELAUS: What then, if not the Assembly?

EURYMACHUS: The people.

DEMOPTOLEMUS: He has a point. What is being proposed is illegal.

ANTINOUS: Demoptolemus, will you tell me what is legal, you?

DEMOPTOLEMUS: You are not the law Antinous, much as you would like to be.

ANTINOUS: And what is the alternative? If we do not respond to this provocation, the Queen will take that as a sign of weakness. In that case, we can reckon on being here simply for ever. And much as that may appeal to some of you here, I for my part seek an end to this, meaning that I am here for a reason, which is not to drink myself into an early grave; it is to obtain the hand of the Queen of this country and to establish a new order in Ithaca.

EURYMACHUS: I believe that her son could discreetly persuade the Queen to arrive at a decision within a given fixed period of time. In that way we can avoid scandal and illegality.

TELEMACHUS: Eurymachus, I never said...

EURYMACHUS: If I am wrong in what I hope for and if Telemachus is not prepared to talk to the Queen or if he fails to convince her, then Antinous will be right and we should have no alternative.
That would mean a scandal and the public humiliation of the monarchy. We should try every alternative before taking such a step.

CTESSIPUS: We do not want a public humiliation of the queen.

DEMOPTOLEMUS: There is another way.

EURYMACHUS: Demoptolemus! I have been trying to overlook you slouching in the corner there. No doubt you have some highly original and entertaining proposals for the selection of the Queen's future husband. And no doubt Ctessipus will be keen to hear what you have to say.

CTESSIPUS: Indeed I should.

EURYMACHUS: Indeed he would.

AMPHINOMUS: Surely the Queen must decide herself whom she marries?

EURYMACHUS: Who will question that? Only Demoptolemus and Agelaus seem

	to think the idea odd, that the queen must decide for herself and in her own time. That is the law and that is the voice of reason.
AGELAUS:	But now she is making fun of us. Her trick with the shroud makes nonsense of the law in any case.
AMPHINOMUS:	She is too sad to make fun of anything or anyone.

(Enter Mentes unnoticed by the suitors)

	She is just waiting for some... *(sees Mentes in the doorway.)* Who's that?
MENTES:	Who is in command here?
ANTINOUS:	I am. And who are you? What do you want? Another suitor? I have issued specific orders that no new suitors be permitted to join us.
CTESSIPUS:	I keep saying. The servants are awful. They let in complete strangers with no warning.
MENTES:	You say you are in command. Then you are the master of this house?
TELEMACHUS:	I am! I am the master of this house.
AGELAUS:	This will be another crank with news of the late King.

CTESSIPUS: Another crank! Another prophet of doom!

EURYMACHUS: This is not the moment, stranger. This is not a time for us to entertain.

TELEMACHUS: Ignore him friend. Be seated. There is still food and wine here.

MENTES: *(Remains standing)* Obviously this is the celebration of some great victory. I did not know that Ithaca had been at war.

ANTINOUS: No war, stranger.

MENTES: No war? Then this feasting is extravagant.

EURYMACHUS: This is not a public feast.

MENTES: *(To Telemachus)* Do you order these?

TELEMACHUS: They are suitors to the Queen. Some have been here for years. Some are more recent. They will not leave, not for a day.

Several suitors loudly: Here to stay! Here to stay! Here to stay!

MENTES: This would not be believed in my home.

AMPHIMEDON: This wine tastes too much of resin. I don't know why it has such a good reputation!

TELEMACHUS: There was a time when you showed respect within these walls.

AMPHIMEDON: Keep calm, I only said I did not greatly like the wine. The cakes are fine.

TELEMACHUS: You plunder the commonwealth and tell me you do not like the wine.

EURYMACHUS: Patience, Telemachus, patience.

TELEMACHUS: I am patient. I am extremely patient. I am the picture of patience. How much longer do I remain patient? And reasonable? And calm? Why, some of these people are not even Ithacan.

ANTINOUS: That is interesting. A fine difference. Are foreign drunkards more unruly than Ithacan originals? Then perhaps you should throw the stranger out, Telemachus. He is obviously foreign.

TELEMACHUS: Who are you?

MENTES: I am Mentes, son of Anchialus from Taphia. I am sailing to the copper mines at Tamesa.

TELEMACHUS:	My mother has often spoken about you. She says that you knew my father. You are welcome here.
MENTES:	And you are Telemachus, his son?
AMPHIMEDON:	We suppose he is!
	(Laughter)
TELEMACHUS:	*(To Mentes)* Let me speak to you apart.
EURYMACHUS:	This is not the time!
ANTINOUS:	Is this a conspiracy? There are no secrets here.
MENTES:	My message is for Telemachus.
ANTINOUS:	Do you know who I am?
MENTES:	No, but I see what you are.
ANTINOUS:	And what am I?
MENTES:	A time waster, a parasite, a doll adored by fools, a man of personal ambition to enrich himself and prosper at the cost of others, a man for whom material benefits and prosperity mean more than the prosperity of the rest of the entire world, be it of Hellas or beyond.

DEMOPTOLEMUS: Concise and to the point.

MENTES: *(Aside to Telemachus)* There is news. News man, news.

TELEMACHUS: Nineteen years and all news has been nothing but false hopes.

MENTES: He is close.

TELEMACHUS: Who?

MENTES: He. He whom you wait for. Your father. The King.

TELEMACHUS: Impossible.

MENTES: Why impossible! I tell you it is so. He is close!

TELEMACHUS: Who has spoken to you?

MENTES: In Sparta, Menelaus. He has heard. Your father was held prisoner by a child of the sea.

TELEMACHUS: I do not understand.

MENTES: The one eyed monster, the Cyclops. You will hear from others soon. Telemachus, what will he think when he returns to this?

TELEMACHUS: That he was too long.

MENTES:

He was too long. That is why you have abandoned faith. You will blame the King for your own weakness, will you?

TELEMACHUS:

I was only a boy when they began. I was only a boy. Melanthius brought them in. He said they were just calling, dropping in to pay their respects to my widowed mother. At the beginning they did not even say widowed, that word came later. It is funny how ably they change language. Later she was my widowed mother, my father, my late father. I never dreamed that they would not move, that they soon began to claim a right to stay. One day there were a few, then more, then suddenly without my noticing, the house was full. And then it was too late.

MENTES:

Blaming others. Now you blame your father's goatherd for your own failing.

TELEMACHUS:

It is true I say. He brought the first suitors to this house.

MENTES:

Melanthius loathed your father but he only succeeded when the state was weak.

TELEMACHUS:

Is it my fault? I was only a child!

MENTES: Will you be able to look your father
               in the face and say that? Will you
               happily say, "Well father, I did the
               best I could".

TELEMACHUS: You think I cannot.

MENTES: We know you cannot. These floors
               which run red with wine, will soon
               be red with their blood.

TELEMACHUS: Murder? But what about the law?

MENTES: The law? Whose law?

TELEMACHUS: The Assembly's, Ithaca's.
               The people's.

MENTES: In the hands of the suitors, of a small
               group of suitors. No law is proposed,
               let alone passed, which is not
               approved by them. That is what the
               world is talking of Telemachus, and
               your shame. The world is talking of
               your shame.
               You know that they have acquired
               great wealth, but how? By subterfuge
               and scheming. They have not
               committed one heroic act.
               They live on the wealth of the past
               but they regard the past with dead
               eyes.
               They consume everything but they
               understand nothing. The world

expected that the King's son would stop them but there has been nothing. Nothing. How can you live with your shame?

TELEMACHUS: Why should I believe you? You have no proof of a return. It is only rumour.

MENTES: How was your father sure that the man who designed this palace could be trusted?

TELEMACHUS: This palace? He designed it himself.

MENTES: How could he trust in others than with a faith in his own ability? And the pillars are firm today. You must have faith.
Fight, fight today, for your father, for Ithaca.

TELEMACHUS: Fight? I cannot fight. I was not trained for any fighting.

MENTES: Call the Assembly. Apply to have them thrown out.

TELEMACHUS: Thrown out!

MENTES: All of them. Now. It is probably too late, I realise that. The legislators are all corrupted by their democracy.

TELEMACHUS: Yes, they are hired men.

MENTES: At least try. Your father otherwise will return and have to say, "and through all these years and through all this time my son was a coward."

TELEMACHUS: I was never challenged. I was never challenged to prove myself.

MENTES: The men are parasites and the women whores. When your father returns, he will destroy them. He will feed them to the pigs. But what of you who has allowed his estate to be milked? Would it be better to die in an attempt than to welcome him as the coward that you are?

TELEMACHUS: You ask me to commit atrocities and to cut throats, you ask me to risk my own life. You urge me to violence without knowing where that violence will lead. It is all hopeless.

MENTES: Not as hopeless as you think. Fate turns the world upside down if the Gods so will. You may have more friends than you know, waiting for a sign, a sign.

TELEMACHUS: For all this I need courage and I have none.

MENTES: To say you have none is the beginning of wisdom and it is the beginning of

courage. Acknowledging cowardice
can be the first act of courage.
Think of your mother. Think of
Achilles.

AGELAUS: The stranger is going. Stranger, did
you tell the boy his father is
returning?
(Exit Mentes)
Did he Telemachus? Was he another
crank full of prophesies and a
coming hullabaloo?

TELEMACHUS: His message was private.

AGELAUS: How mysterious. But you heard
Antinous. No secrets. No secrets
any more! So tell us, what did he
want?

TELEMACHUS: He was talking about the pigs.

ANTINOUS: Pigs?

TELEMACHUS: He said that I should feed them
better.

AGELAUS: A swineherd.

AMPHINOMUS: Someone who works for that
sorceress from Aiaia. . .

TELEMACHUS: He talked like a God... His eyes...
Antinous, I think the Assembly
should be convened.

ANTINOUS: A welcome change of heart. Do you hear, Eurymachus? Even Telemachus agrees with us now.

EURYMACHUS: I am amazed. Do you realise what will they say about the shroud?

TELEMACHUS: Not because of the shroud. Although there may be a question of shrouds.

AGELAUS: What do you mean, what are you talking about? This is all about the shroud. Your mother's tricks because she will not accept the inevitable and marry again.

ANTINOUS: Not the shroud, then what?

TELEMACHUS: A motion of ejection.

ANTINOUS: Ejection? You want to propose our ejection? That's not very democratic.

TELEMACHUS: I do not know whether it is democratic or not. The fact is that you do not belong here. None of you. This is not your house.

AGELAUS: A conspiracy against democracy, but the prince does not have the brains to plan it. Eurymachus is behind this!

AMPHINOMUS: Or the stranger.

EURYMACHUS: What possible interest could I have in any such thing?

PEISANDER:	You can't make us go. We have a right to be here!
EURYMACHUS:	Telemachus, you have been badly advised.
AMPHINOMUS:	Who was the stranger?
TELEMACHUS:	His eyes…
EURYMACHUS:	His eyes? What of them?
TELEMACHUS:	I could not look away!
EURYMACHUS:	It is well known that the Gods sometimes assume a human shape. This guest was none other than Pallas Athene.
AGELAUS:	A plot! A plot! I told you! They are in this together!
EURYMACHUS:	*(Aside to Agelaus)* Quiet you fool! Yes, I am certain this was Pallas Athene. She wants you to act, Telemachus.
TELEMACHUS:	Yes, yes yes! To act!
EURYMACHUS:	Did she mention your father?
TELEMACHUS:	Yes.
ANTINOUS:	Eurymachus, I don't see…

EURYMACHUS: What did she say?

TELEMACHUS: Menelaus of Sparta. I am already forgetting. Something about Menelaus of Sparta.

EURYMACHUS: You must go to see him. Find out what exactly he knows.

TELEMACHUS: And the Assembly?

CTESSIPUS: We demand satisfaction from your mother. She's juggling with us. She is a fraud.

EURYMACHUS: *(Aside to Ctessipus)* Silence you fool!

PEISANDER: She is full of lies and evasions.

EURYMACHUS: Stop them Antinous. They are mad.

ANTINOUS: It seems to me that it is you who have become mad, Eurymachus. I agree with them.

CTESSIPUS: First we wait for her to finish a shroud which will never, never be finished and now her son proposes to disappear to Sparta, obviously to stir up trouble there.

AGELAUS: Encouraged by Eurymachus!

PEISANDER: More waiting.

CTESSIPUS: It's not good enough.

EURYMACHUS: You won't make her change now.
She does not have to decide!

AGELAUS: We shall make her decide!

EURYMACHUS: Make her decide what?

ANTINOUS: We all want a decision, Eurymachus.
Our patience is at an end. Only you
seem happy to continue waiting.

AGELAUS: I sometimes wonder if Eurymachus
is a real democrat.

DEMOPTOLEMUS: Nobody here is a democrat! There is
no democracy in any state.

EURYMACHUS: This is all irrelevant.

AGELAUS: We would expect you to say so. Most
of us are not here to lead a pampered
life but to marry a beautiful woman.

EURYMACHUS: Are you questioning my honesty
Agelaus?

AGELAUS: Your what? Your wings?

TELEMACHUS: You should all go, all of you, all of
you!

(Exit Telemachus)

EURYMACHUS: Not clever Antinous, not clever at all. Badly managed. Congratulations everybody! You will have the uproar and publicity which you obviously crave.

POLYBOS: Antinous knows best, not you. You have become extremely clever, Eurymachus, but you have forgotten that you are only a spokesman, only a spokesman.

EURYMACHUS: Father, you are wrong. The vote could turn against us.

ANTINOUS: How can it?

AGELAUS: All the Assembly is with us, excepting Mentor and a handful of others.

PEISANDER: If he calls the Assembly, the world will see his weakness and decline.

AMPHINOMUS: If the Assembly is called, he will feel his arguments have some legitimacy.

EURYMACHUS: Any publicity is good publicity for him. That is why this should have been prevented.

AGELAUS: We shall remind the Assembly of his father's tyranny.

EURYMACUS: Amphinomus, see there is no one at the door.

(Amphinomus goes to door)

AMPHINOMUS:	There is nobody there.
EURYMACHUS:	I have a suggestion to make.
AMPHIMEDON:	We'll tell the Assembly about the atrocious wine here too.
EURYMACHUS:	Can we please be serious?
AGELAUS:	You have had your turn. It is my turn now. Will Telemachus be allowed to speak at all?
ANTINOUS:	What do you mean Agelaus? How can we stop him speaking on his own motion?
AGELAUS:	There is an edict, is there not, approved by you at the time Antinous, contested by no one in the Assembly but Mentor, disallowing anyone from speaking in favour of tyranny from addressing the Assembly.
ANTINOUS:	I know the edict well of course. Unfortunately this issue is concerned with property and Telemachus will be heard.
DEMOPTOLEMUS:	Are you sure? He is the son of Odysseus, he is the son of his tyrant father. That is enough to disallow him.

EURYMACHUS: Will you please let me speak?

ANTINOUS: Very well, Eurymachus, speak. Explain your strange behaviour. Why do you want to allow Telemachus to speak in front of the Assembly? And why did you turn against Ctessipus?

CTESSIPUS: It is normal. He likes to take sides with the boy. He always does.

EURYMACHUS: It would be better he sailed for Sparta. Don't you see? The Assembly might not have been necessary. Poseidon hates Odysseus. The seas are perilous. If he had gone to Sparta...

ANTINOUS: He might have only gone, you mean?

EURYMACHUS: He might only have gone.

CTESSIOPUS: In the meantime we would be waiting.

EURYMACHUS: If the news had then come to us that he had drowned like his father, or if he had been attacked on the voyage by pirates and slain, then the Queen would be ours.

ANTINOUS: Ours?

EURYMACHUS: Or yours or mine or anyone's. But that is all if and had. The fact is that the Assembly will be called and you have added passion to the passion which the stranger gave him.

PEISANDER: I did not trust that stranger.

AMPHIMEDON: It's a pity that the stranger did not drink; he might have poisoned himself on the filthy wine.

ANTINOUS: Eurymachus, I should never underestimate you. We shall no doubt be called to the Assembly soon. When that is all over, Eurymachus will ensure that Telemachus does take the promised trip to Sparta. There is no knowing how Poseidon will feel about that. As for Her Majesty, no one can deny that the time has been finally reached when she must announce her choice and bring the chaos of the current state to an end.

Act Two Scene One

The shoreline of Ogygia.

Odysseus seated on a stone, gazing out to sea. Behind him stands Calypso.

ODYSSEUS: He triumphs in this defeat.

CALYPSO: You blinded his only son. A God wills your destruction. Poseidon's son is dead and his rage unappeasable.

ODYSSEUS: But his rage against me existed before my crew was captured by his son. Being captured by his son, our escape, our blinding of his son, was not the first cause of Poseidon's rejection. Even before I blinded that wild shepherd giant, Poseidon hated me. From the moment I set sail to return, I have been cursed; he threw me up here to slowly....

CALYPSO: Slowly what?

ODYSSEUS: Slowly become inanimate.

CALYPSO: A very strange choice of words, considering that I have offered cunning Odysseus immortality.

ODYSSEUS: Immortal imprisonment, that is
your immortality. There are no
visible bars but it is a prison. Your
island is like a prison to me. No, it is
not like a prison, it is my prison.

CALYPSO: You are ungrateful. I found you
nearly drowned. I nursed you back
to life.
You seemed grateful then. Was that
an illusion of a lonely woman?

ODYSSEUS: I am grateful for the rescue, of
course I am but I will not permit
you to use that as a reason for
holding me a prisoner here for ever.
I had rather then not been saved. I
shall leave you whatever you desire
and you will not stop me, unless as
an immortal you can stop me and
then you must kill me.
Either way, you will not hold me
here like some caged bird for your
entertainment.
Every man has an instinct, a drive.
My instinct told me, "man, you are
saved!" so yes, I was grateful and
therefore I felt indebted.
I had forgotten, not for long, but for
a short time I had forgotten and in
that time of forgetting I felt
indebted. That time was short.
Now I remember again. Now I see
again. I see, I see myself, I see you,

but I cannot understand why I
cannot see the land.

CALYPSO: What do you mean? You can see
me, you can see your hands and you
can see here before you, this land.

ODYSSEUS: My land, my land, I cannot see my
land, I cannot see Ithaca. Over the
wine dark sea we should see a
horizon. There is nothing between
us. We see the stars and how far
away are they? No man knows but
surely further by many leagues than
Ithaca? I see the stars, why cannot I
see Ithaca?
Why does the God of the sea so
despise me? Why? He despised me
long before his son captured us. It
cannot be that alone. Is it for some
fault of mine which I cannot see in
myself? Have I not made sacrifices
enough? But I have made sacrifices.
I have always observed all the rites.
Is it that my heart was not there? If
we make a sacrifice and our heart is
not in what we do, is the sacrifice
worthless? Is not only the sea but
fate against me? Perhaps that too I
shall only learn after my return.

CALYPSO: Then my sacrifice was worthless,
my sacrifice to save you, to feed
you. You cannot forget her.

ODYSSEUS: I have half forgotten her.

CALYPSO: I can hardly picture her, nor can I
picture this forgotten or half-
dreamed land you rave about.
I cannot understand why you
should care what drives Poseidon
on, or why he loaded the future
against you. You say you will return,
but where to?
Some Ithaca of a distant past, that is
what you are returning to and that
is what you will not find, Odysseus.
Time does not return. Not even the
Gods can do that. Time is beyond
even the Gods.
Time is now and home is where you
live and thrive. Your home now is
Ogygia. In Ogygia you will become
immortally at peace. If you leave
me, you will perish, oh maybe not
immediately; you may escape
Poseidon, but you will perish all
the same. You will be mortal again
and in a few years you will perish
and enter into oblivion.
Can you even begin to imagine
the meaning of oblivion?
Oblivion!

ODYSSEUS: What you call peace is not peace for
me but a tedium and a guilty
conscience. I have no right to stay
here. I have a duty to return.

CALYPSO: The cycles of nature have been broken, violently broken. It will break your stony male heart and you will weep like a girl.

ODYSSEUS: Whatever I find I must face and if necessary I must fight.

CALYPSO: Fight? For what?

ODYSSEUS: For the restoration.

CALYPSO: The restoration? What restoration?

ODYSSEUS: The restoration of a natural order, to repair the harvest and the cycle, to heal the dying, to restore harmony. I am returning to restore harmony to a world which is losing all harmony and is falling under a shadow. The restoration of our race.

CALYPSO: You may fail.

ODYSSEUS: If you say so, then I know I may but you cannot reverse my will in any way. I must attempt it. I have been here as though I were all the while asleep, as though you had drugged me into a forgetfulness. I do not blame you. You too have a role but now I see mine clearly. I do not know exactly how or why. Perhaps it was the memory of the hunts in the forest or the blue rock doves of Ithaca or the olive trees or our fine wine or the swallows returning every summer, perhaps it was the faces of the girls returning from harvest, days as though the sun shone every day and no ungrateful parasites disgraced the land, or maybe it is simply the frustration that I cannot see my land from where I am; or maybe it is intuition that I must leave, the awareness now that time is running out, that if I do not leave now it will be too late, that the new order of death which can be imposed like a creeping sickness to death will have become irrevocable.

Maybe it is a sudden guilty conscience. I have a wife and that wife is waiting, waiting. I have lost count of the days but she must surely have waited years.

Nothing you can say can change me. You saved my life. How can I not be grateful to you? But I do not belong here.

CALYPSO:

I knew I would fail. I knew that I would not be enough, nor this peace, nor the promise of immortality. I have been ten times more beautiful than any mortal you have seen.

You said as much yourself. Dare I say I am more beautiful than she? And unlike your wife, I do not age.

ODYSSEUS: I belong in time. The golden age when men could see a world not held in time, is past, is itself time-destroyed, time-unmade. I am made of the clay and dust and dirt of unendurable hard land and soil. I am not a goddess or a god, I am a man of Ithaca, I am king of Ithaca. I was given her in trust. I have sinned in my lateness but staying with you is to sin more, every day is to sin more!
Ithaca is a home, a homeland which means nothing to you just as Ogygia will seem nothing to me when I no longer see the coastline of your island. With all your luxury you give me nothing more than peace, not even peace, for I am unsettled by my call, my duty. A voice tells me, again and again, more and more bitingly, more and more persistently, "you have been away too long, too long you so-called king of Ithaca."

CALYPSO: My island you will soon forget that it restored you to life. You turn your back on the place which gave you new life. Why did I pity you when I

found you on the shore exhausted,
your lungs full of sea salt?
Why did I take you to my home?
Why did I restore you to your
strength?

ODYSSEUS: I have no way of repaying you.
              I have nothing to offer you.

CALYPSO: You have your beauty, Odysseus,
              your company.

ODYSSEUS: So even Gods are lonely?

CALYPSO: Even Gods want to contemplate
              their creation. You have your
              world. What have I? You could
              have pitied me.

ODYSSEUS: A mortal pity a Goddess!

CALYPSO: Immortal, we are still vulnerable.

ODYSSEUS: The Gods cannot die, so what do
              you mean "vulnerable"?

CALYPSO: Men speak of immortal Gods but
              the Gods live from the love of the
              mortals whom they have created.
              Without their love, they...perish.
              When I found you, I thought that
              Poseidon had taken pity on me,
              pitied my loneliness. I offered you
              so much.

ODYSSEUS: Should I apologize? I did not want your offer of immortality in ignorance.

CALYPSO: A small consolation Odysseus. I thought Poseidon had brought me a gift.

ODYSSEUS: A gift.

CALYPSO: Of peace and immortality. The Golden Age again. Here. Just here.

ODYSSEUS: Peace and immortality. Fruitless gifts! To be close to defeat, close to death is to be close to life. I live in time. I live to feel the thrust of life and death and the cold breath of the sea which I fear and cannot leave.

CALYPSO: You will go and forget me completely.

ODYSSEUS: No mortal remains for ever, you said so yourself. We do not want to belong to one place for ever.

CALYPSO: Then you do not even belong to Ithaca forever?

ODYSSEUS: It is there.

CALYPSO: What is there?

ODYSSEUS: Death, naturally.

CALYPSO: If it is only death....

ODYSSEUS: No, no. It is not only death. It is
                            fulfilment. It is what must be
                            completed. I shall return to my son
                            and to my wife.

CALYPSO: Do you not ask yourself, how will
                            things have been changed? It is a
                            long time.

ODYSSEUS: There are the cycles of time. My
                            wife will be older. Or do you know
                            more? My son and wife, are they
                            still well?

CALYPSO: I have been concealing from you...

ODYSSEUS: Concealing?

CALYPSO: Odysseus, there are new men in
                            Ithaca. They are erecting the
                            faceless towers of a new order. Even
                            Zeus trembles before their...

ODYSSEUS: Their what, Calypso?

CALYPSO: Their soulessness. They seem to
                            have no souls at all and their
                            towers are blank, dead lines of
                            naked rock which shimmers in the
                            harsh light and offers nothing, not
                            even fear, simply nothing.
                            Something like oblivion.

ODYSSEUS: Sacrilege. I knew it. I could not see
             but I could sense it.

CALYPSO: They respect nothing of what was
             yours. They are destroying the
             forests with their goats. Only the
             stunted hermes oak grows on the
             hillsides now. The palace courtyard
             is a pigsty.
             The palace handmaids have been
             debauched with your own silver.
             The craftsmen of Ithaca beg in the
             streets. Lacklustre parasites feed in
             the orchards. The land is turning
             from green to grey.

ODYSSEUS: For pity's sake, enough! No, one
             thing more, can you see? Is my wife
             unhurt?

CALYPSO: I do not see her. The Gods bring no
             news of her, neither good nor bad.
             There is a sort of screen around her.

ODYSSEUS: Too long! Too long! Too long! I
             must go.

CALYPSO: You will go.

ODYSSEUS: Ithaca offers me freedom.

CALYPSO: Or Ithaca will bring you death.
             Beyond the confines of my magic
             here, death will be in the very

atoms of the air you breathe into
your lungs. Beyond my island, you
walk in death and you breathe it, all
around you.

ODYSSEUS: My wanderings were aimless if they
did not lead me home to Ithaca. I
have been too long, too long!

CALYPSO: Within time.

ODYSSEUS: Say that by what I do I shall change
the very course of time and how
can even the greatest among us
better challenge time and wrestle
with time than in that way?
Would you have me stay and hear
how my son and my wife and my
land are all destroyed?

CALYPSO: We know Ithaca differently. I see in
my mind's eye a rock with too many
goats. A few birds. A couple of olive
trees. You see some kind of Elysium
although it is an Elysium in time.

ODYSSEUS: I see the same as you but I have
other eyes, other mind's eyes. I
have no illusions after the Golden
Age, of perfection. We are plagued
by sea squalls in Ithaca. They seem
to come from nowhere on fine days
and when they come everything is
blown away that we have not

fastened. Goats are blown off their feet. Trees are uprooted. The sea becomes murderous and wild. The people become foul mouthed and distrustful.

CALYPSO: You will return to that? You will return to that tawdriness, that waste and sadness and pain and all under indifferent eyes and under an indifferent sky?

ODYSSEUS: I must.

CALYPSO: Why? Why must you?

ODYSSEUS: Because, for better or for worse, Ithaca is my beloved country.

CALYPSO: Your country! Your country! What does that even mean under heaven? Your beloved country will forget you when you die. It did not know you once. It will not know you when you have come to the river. Your country? Are you an owner? As king you own the land? Is that your meaning? Do you mean that you own the country, this Ithaca, this windy rock you rave about?

ODYSSEUS: We do not own the country.

CALYPSO: What then?

ODYSSEUS: The country owns us. We Ithacans
            make Ithaca what she is and will be.
            Yesterday and tomorrow's children
            have tilled the soil and planted trees
            there.
            I cherish every part of that land
            which is theirs and ours.
            From what you say, Ithaca today
            is in a kind of darkness, but that
            time will pass. One day our
            children shall cry rejoicing because
            the dear homeland is ours once
            more.

CALYPSO: If you safely return and if you
            succeed in driving out the looters,
            yet you will not stay. You will not
            bring her the peace she expects.
            You are glorious in your struggles,
            your wars. In times of peace you
            feel that you will stagnate.

ODYSSEUS: I could imagine no cause to leave
            again.

CALYPSO: No? Then why did you sail away in
            the first place?

ODYSSEUS: The war in Ilios brought honour.

CALYPSO: And blood and great pain.

ODYSSEUS: Yes, yes you are right. It brought
            blood, pain and anguish.

CALYPSO: Anguish! What do you know of anguish? You cannot tell me why you left, can you? And you cannot tell her.

ODYSSEUS: We have suffered from the same, Calypso.

CALYPSO: And that is?

ODYSSEUS: Unrequited love.

CALYPSO: You think she does not love you?

ODYSSEUS: She does not love me as I love her. I was her source of strength and her protector and provider but she...I have never been...She has never...

CALYPSO: Loved you?

ODYSSEUS: She has needed me, sometimes I think as a spider needs its mate.

CALYPSO: And you will return to her? You will return to this doubtful wife when you could be happy here with me?

ODYSSEUS: If she does not recognise me, I will leave her at once.

CALYPSO: It is said that when a mortal is dying all the memories of the short life which was his return in procession before his fading sight, including much that he had forgotten. If Ithaca is dying, it is now that she will remember you.

ODYSSEUS: If you can see so much, can you tell me, honestly, shall I find victory in Ithaca?

CALYPSO: Victory is within you, Odysseus.

ODYSSEUS: Within me? How should I understand that?

CALYPSO: If your will is strong enough to rectify fate, then you may be victorious. That is for you to say, not for me.

ODYSSEUS: Then tell me at least, how will they receive me? My son I mean, my people and my wife.

CALYPSO: The people with dead eyes, your son with shame and unbelief and your wife, I cannot say.

ODYSSEUS: Indifferently? Horrible! Indifference is worse than hatred!

CALYPSO: They have no poetry in their hearts. They no longer sing. The land is loud yet silent, my friend, and every day louder and more silent. When they see you, they will wait to see your strength tested and when they see you strong they will accept you, but their eyes will be cold, indifferent, just accepting.

ODYSSEUS: You lie to tempt me to stay!

CALYPSO: No!

ODYSSEUS: Oh yes, a trick. They love me! Indifference. Dear Gods: not indifference, not not caring, not not looking, not not fearing. Indifference is the darkest hand, most terrible of all.

CALYPSO: It is the fate of all mortals, the indifference of the very earth. The rocks and trees will not care if Odysseus returns, and if he returns, how he will be greeted. No thunder will sound in the sky marking the return of a king.

ODYSSEUS: But I greet that indifferent earth, for it is my earth, the earth that I love! I will return! I will return! I will return! To the land I love. Heavenly God, the land I love. I have been fed on lies. They have told me the land does not matter. The land matters, the land, the land!

CALYPSO: And the indifference, how will you fight that?

ODYSSEUS: Indifference? I had rather that the children of Ithaca stone me in the streets and the rabble call me tyrant or traitor or both and hang me on a cross than they should ignore me.

CALYPSO: What conceit! Do you have such a high opinion of yourself?

ODYSSEUS: Is my opinion not justified?

CALYPSO: You ask me? I can only tell you what I see.

ODYSSEUS: One voice will be enough, one young voice to proclaim me. To proclaim the King's return and the King's glory! Then all will see me.

CALYPSO: So you need the admiration of others to thrive? Are you not self-sufficient, confident enough of what you yourself can achieve? Is that not a parasite life with its dependence on the approval and giving of others?

ODYSSEUS: What I take I give back. No king rules, no governor rules, no tyrant rules without an inner compliance. A tyrant once ignored is powerless.

CALYPSO: Still there are tyrants. On every coast there are tyrants.

ODYSSEUS: But not by force alone.

CALYPSO: Are you not afraid of what could happen? You are returning without an army, not even with armed companions. You are returning over a doubtful sea completely alone.

ODYSSEUS: I fear more the unborn and the dead. I am afraid to meet them across the river, to meet them all and hear them whispering.
"Now here comes the Traitor King. Hello Traitor King, the one who denied his Faith and Land."
"Now comes the Coward King."
And that reproach for ever, for ever, for ever! That will not happen, nor defeat. I am returning like the swallows of summer. If I die, I will die knowing I did my best.

CALYPSO: How very touching. It sounds like a report of a mediocre school boy's progress. "He tried hard. He did his very best."
Not good enough, Odysseus. You must be recognised. You must have one who sees you and accepts you at once without condition, without needing a sign, one who knows at once. You are full of fine poetry but who can be sure how you will prove? Like the swallows of

summer, are you? And how do the swallows of summer return to Ithaca?

ODYSSEUS: They return predictably, inevitably.

CALYPSO: But if all their old nesting homes are blocked they are confounded. Ithaca is not what she was. The land is covered in forgetfulness.

ODYSSEUS: Then if I die, say I was her fate Calypso. I am her fate. I cannot abandon my duty. Nothing you say will deter me. Quite the reverse.

CALYPSO: Leave them to their fate. They will not thank you.

ODYSSEUS: Do that and you deprive them of the light, your father's very gift to you. You deprive them of the sun. I was born to conquer. Men live not only with their ambitions, they live through them.

CALYPSO: I am tired of arguing. You are stubborn and you will embrace what you call your fate. Then go quickly and greet this fate you are so impatient to meet.

ODYSSEUS: First I need your help. Practical help. My ships have been destroyed.

I need to find good timber, ropes
canvas. I need supplies, water,
fruit and bread.

CALYPSO: You will have your help.

ODYSSEUS: Thank you Calypso.

CALYPSO: You do not have to thank me. You
have your future and I have now
an almost mortal past. In your arms
I discovered what the gods hardly
know.

ODYSSEUS: Being?

CALYPSO: Human love of course, the choosing
of one insignificant mortal among
millions and endowing that mortal
with the qualities of a God. Answer
one last question and then I shall
have no more.

ODYSSEUS: Willingly.

CALYPSO: Were you happy here, with me,
playing the role of an immortal?

ODYSSEUS: If I escape Poseidon again, will the
rest be easy or will another God bar
my way?

CALYPSO: You said you would answer my last
question, so tell me, tell me you
were happy!

ODYSSEUS: Clytemnestra welcomed her husband home from war with open arms...

CALYPSO: Look at me!

ODYSSEUS: Will my son laugh at me? Will he even recognise me? Will I recognise him? Hardly. He was so young. Will I recognise him with instinct or will someone have to say, will my wife have to say, "he is yours"?

CALYPSO: Did you love me?

ODYSSEUS: I long to see these so-called suitors. I shall not spare one.

CALYPSO: You are forgetting me already. You are indifferent. We shall all perish, perish through our love of mankind. We shall all perish. The Gods will perish.

ODYSSEUS: I shall ignore hardship and overcome. My poor homeland, so long delayed, so long delayed, the homecoming king. Pallas Athene protect me. Almighty Zeus, whose life is a paradigm of ours, show me the righteousness of my vengeance and the justice of my struggle. Sanctify my blood offering. Bless my home coming. Bless the hero's return.

CALYPSO: Odysseus, if you say nothing to me
             now, you leave under my curse!

ODYSSEUS: *(Slowly turning towards her,*
             recognising her with difficulty, then
             with an effort, speaking to her:)
             Without you, this would have been
             impossible. Without you my body
             would now be one with the sand
             and the sea and the waves and my
             spirit would be grieving for the
             unaccomplished destiny of
             Odysseus on the other side of the
             unspeakable river.

CALYPSO: Go with....

ODYSSEUS: Go? Yes? Go! Go? With? With?

CALYPSO: With my blessing, go with my
             blessing, Odysseus, my blessing as
             a curse but still my love.

ODYSSEUS: So long and too long, but now the
             leaves are stirring in the trees and
             the water is stirring and the beasts
             are uneasy, they that first sense a
             change when the sky seems clear
             and the towers of despoilers'
             iniquity glitter like gold in the
             unsmiling sunlight. The hurricane
             is close.

             (Exeunt)

Act Two Scene Two

The Ithacan Assembly

Aegyptius is seated at the centre of the room; on either side of him are members of the Assembly, including all the suitors, also Mentor, Halitherses and Telemachus.

AEGYPTIUS: This meeting of the Assembly of the people of Ithaca has been gathered in extraordinary session to hear a complaint brought by Telemachus, by the son of the late King...

HALITHERSES: Late King? Late? How dare you say so!

EURYMACHUS: Halitherses, you are drunk again. Show respect in this place, or I shall have you evicted.

AEGYPTIUS: Thank you. Now, where was I?

ANTNIOUS: Late king!

AEGYPTIUS: Ah yes, indeed. Late king... against the suitors currently residing at his father's house.

EURYMACHUS: Pardon me, there is a mistake there.

AEGYPTIUS: A mistake, young man?

AGELAUS: Just get on with it!

AEGYPTIUS: No no, if there is a mistake, even of a technical nature, any decision taken by this Assembly may be later challenged. I ask again young man, what mistake?

EURYMACHUS: Only some of us are currently resident in the palace. Others are occasional visitors. My father and I, for instance, rarely sleep there.

POLYBOS: That's right. When the feasting has finished for the day, many of us, my son and I for example, walk home.

AGELAUS: Stagger home, you mean!

POLYBOS: My home is not far from the palace. I am not even at the palace every day. On some days I have other business to attend to.

EURYMACHUS: So I propose that we change the wording of the complaint to read, "Against those suitors permanently resident at his father's house."

CTESSIPUS: Not so fast. That would alter the meaning. Then those not resident are not part of the complaint.

TELEMACHUS: My complaint, I assure you, is against all the suitors, not just those who sleep at my father's house, but against all of them, every one of them.

EURYMACHUS: Very well, then. Then the complaint should read, "a complaint brought by Telemachus against all his mother's suitors."

AGELAUS: Legalistic hair-splitting!

AMPHIMEDON: All suitors, all over the world. A complaint against suitors.

TELEMACHUS: I am bringing a complaint. I am proposing a motion.

AEGYPTIUS: Telemachus, proposing motions is my duty as president of the Assembly.

TELAMACHUS: I am bringing a complaint against everyone currently resident or visiting my father's house.

(*Laughter, interruptions*)

AMPHIMEDON: What, even the beggars?

AGELAUS: Even against himself?

ANTINOUS: Even against his mother? Against his mother? Perhaps according to his hostile and hate-filled plea, his mother should leave the palace.

After all, it his mother who is the cause of all the trouble we have. If it had not been for his mother and his mother's famous, or should I say infamous, delays, there would be no suitors in the palace of his lamented father.

TELEMACHUS: Visiting my father's house...

(More interruptions, catcalls, laughter)

AEGYPTIUS: Order! Order! Shall I read this out? Is this what I am to read out?

AMPHIMEDON: Yes, yes, read it out.

PEISANDER: Get on with it!

DEMOPTOLEMOS: Show some respect!

EURYMACHUS: Respect? That is impudent coming from the man of no respect, the anarchist, Demoptolemus.

ANTINOUS: Aegyptius, read out the complaint as it has just been registered by Telemachus, son of the late king.

AEGYPTIUS: Willingly, when I am permitted to speak.

AGELAUS: Quiet, everyone!

AMPHIMEDON: We are listening.

AEGYPTIUS: Then I can begin. The meeting of the Assembly of Ithaca has been gathered.

EURYMACHUS: Is gathered, not has been gathered. The difference is subtle but important.

AEGELAUS: It is too subtle for me.

ANTINOUS: Let him get on with it, Eurymachus, or we shall be here for the rest of the day and half the night too. That is the second time that you have made a pointless interruption.

POLYBOS: His interruption was not pointless, Antinous.

ANTINOUS: Polybos, with respect, you know nothing of constitutional procedure.

POLYBOS: But my son does.

AEGYPTIUS: I am reading the complaint as I heard it from the plaintiff himself and I shall repeat it as I heard it. The meeting of the Assembly of the people of Ithaca has been gathered...

EURYMACHUS: Is gathered!

ANTINOUS:	Ignore him and proceed.
AEGYPTIUS:	I shall, I shall indeed…has been gathered…er…to hear a particular complaint brought by Telemachus…
DEMOPTOLEMOS:	Who?
ANTINOUS:	By Poseidon, let him get on with it!
AEGYPTIUS:	Brought by Telemachus, I say, son of the late king..
DEMOPTOLEMOS:	Oh him!
AEGYPTIUS:	A complaint brought by our late king, no I mean of course by the son of our late king, against those suitors currently resident at my father's house.

(General hilarity, catcalls, laughter)

AGELAUS:	His father's house you fool, not yours!
AMPHIMEDON:	His father is dead. You should say, the widow's palace; or the house of bad wine.
ANTINOUS:	Resident at his father's house! His father's house.
AGELAUS:	Visiting, not just resident.
AEGYPTIUS:	Quite right indeed, visiting or

resident at his father's house for the purpose of seeking the hand of his mother in matrimony.

ANTINOUS: The meaning is very clear.

PEISANDER: Yes, the swine.

AMPHIMEDON: And what is the complaint? What are we supposed to have done? We are just exercising our rights!

Loud cries amounting to a barrage from several voices: Suitors' rights! Suitors' rights! Suitors' rights!

AEGYPTIUS: Telemachus, speak first.

(Telemachus advances)

TELEMACHUS: Odysseus, my father.

AMPHIMEDON: Late father!

PEISANDER: Late, late father. Odysseus, the King who came too late!

TELEACHUS: Once, or maybe now still, king of Ithaca, is, as you all know, lost...

AMPHIMEDON: And presumed missing.

PEISANDER: Missing, but not missed!

TELEMACHUS: Abroad, lost abroad, lost without trace, without anyone knowing

what has become of him, lost to
view and tale, while returning from
the war against the city of Ilios.
We cannot be sure, neither you nor
I nor anyone, whether he is trying
to return and repeatedly prevented,
whether he has lost his way entirely,
whether he has fallen in some fight,
succumbed to some disease, the
victim of fate or some God's whim.
You all know him to have been a
just ruler...

PEISANDER: A tyrant and exploiter, so he was
known!

TELEMACHUS: His wife, my mother is beleaguered
by suitors.

EURYMACHUS: Beleaguered! A strong word that.
Beleaguered is an exaggeration.

TELEMACHUS: By suitors not one of whom she has
said she wants to marry.

PEISANDER: But she must! She must! She must
marry!

Voices: Suitors' rights! Suitors' rights!

AMPHIMEDON: Correct!

TELEMACHUS: She claims my father is alive. It is
the grounds for her not marrying.
These men are not at all put out by
my mother's hope.

They claim they have a right to stay
here so long as she does not pick
one of them to father a new breed.

PEISANDER: Father a new breed! What do you
make of that language!

AMPHIMEDON: He condemns himself out of his
own mouth. It's unbelievable!

TELEMACHUS: At first they came just to visit, or so
they said, but soon it was clear they
were here to stay.
To stay for ever, it seems to me. We
were told at the beginning that they
would pay a visit occasionally and
leave then for their own homes.
So it was for a while, a short while,
but in time some of them chose not
to return to their homes for the
night. They slept the night where
drunkenness had taken them,
inebriate, sprawled across the
tables. Subsequently, some came to
stay the night and we were told that
they would only occasionally stay
the night, now this occasionally has
become a permanently.
They stay and sleep where they fall,
drunken, uncaring, debauched.
They are wasting my inheritance.

EURYMACHUS: Objection. If, as he implies, his
mother is not a widow, then it is
not yet his inheritance.

TELEMACHUS: I hold my father's fortune in trust. You will all disinherit me. That is what you want to do.

ANTINOUS: Telemachus, please, nobody has threatened you, nobody has said please leave, nobody has questioned your right to remain here.

TELEMACHUS: Some of these suitors are not even from Ithaca at all.

AGELAUS: What has that got to do with it?

ANTINOUS: Xenophobia, charming, that's all we need.

PEISANDER: It is the kind of thing we might expect him to dredge up.

TELEMACHUS: Agelaus is a foreigner and so is Amphinomous.

PEISANDER: Is that relevant in any way to what you are trying to say, Telemachus?

TELEMACHUS: The wealth of my father's house is being plundered!

ANTINOUS: Just a minute. Telemachus, is there something especially displeasing to you about the fact that some of the suitors for your mother's hand are not from the island of Ithaca? Does their accent bother you? Do you not like the way they dress? Do you imagine that they turn into wolves by the light of the full moon? Are they, as you see it, less intelligent, or less cultivated, less civilized than Ithacans, are they practically speaking, barbarians, non-men? The Assembly has a right to know how you feel, I hesitate to say think, because such responses are not matters of serious thought at all. I am so intrigued that Telemachus has a prejudice towards those suitors coming from outside Ithaca.

EURYMACHUS: This language is ill-advised, Telemachus. Man, you are your own worst enemy.

TELEMACHUS: Ithaca is being ransacked.

AMPHIMEDON: Not just the palace now, all Ithaca, by foreigners. It is an invasion! Oh dear! Where are my weapons? We must fight the enemy, the big bad invader. Oh look, these nasty foreigners are taking away my jobs, they are going to sleep with my daughter! Oh I am afraid! I am so afraid! That is the language of the little man Telemachus, the little man.

AGELAUS: What have you got against foreigners, Telemachus?

TELEMACHUS: I did not say that I was against foreigners. I am against the suitors. You are all looters!

AGELAUS: And if we are, and if we are... which we are not, then you and your family have only got themselves to blame. You taught us by example that wealth belongs to the strong. We are only pupils of your late father, the proudest looter ever to have been born an Ithacan! The place is groaning under the loot he brought home from countless wars.

TELEMACHUS: He fought for what he obtained.

DEMOPTOLEMOS: Obtained! That's what they call it now! Obtained!

AGELAUS: And I will fight for what I want to have. By that argument we have the right here to kill you and help ourselves. Looting just as your father looted.
You should be grateful we now have democratic law. We believe that a man should become wealthy only through peaceful methods, not through war.

DEMOPTOLEMOS: Peaceful methods are war too! The distinction is entirely misleading. We are at war with the rich.

AGELAUS: Money is made, or should be made, through honest negotiations and barter.

TELEMACHUS: You are happy, all of you, to enjoy the fruits of what Agelaus calls looted wealth.

DEMOPTOLEMOS: There he has a point. Antinous thinks he can limit the late tyrant's wealth to a coterie of chosen landowners, but the land's wealth belongs to everyone, everyone and not just a handful of suitors for Penelope's old hand!

TELEMACHUS: The people are complaining. They are weary of this government.

AMPHIMEDON: Your kind of people, not ours.

EURYMACHUS: Can we return to the original complaint?

TELEMACHUS: Very well. No suitor has a right to stay in my father's palace.

PEISANDER: The suitors have every right, every right!

HALITHERSES: No right! Throw them out! All of them! Throw them out!

AEGYPTIUS: It would make my task easier if both sides in this dispute showed more respect to the chair.

Telemachus, the right is written and confirmed by law.

TELEMACHUS: Made and passed by them!

AEGYPTIUS: Well of course, it is a democratic decision. I hope you are not questioning the validity of the decisions of the democratic Assembly of Ithaca.

ANTINOUS: Aegyptius, I fear you are old and naïve. That is exactly what he is doing. Some people still do not believe in democracy at all. They want to impose tyranny upon us.

AGELAUS: He is no republican!

AEGYPTIUS: Not believe in democracy! No republican. You exaggerate. Of course he believes in democracy. Of course he is a republican. Everyone is republican these days, you know.

AGELAUS: If you could read into his soul you would read that he despises democracy and longs for the destruction of the republic.

DEMOPTOLEMOS: True. His father was a tyrant and it is in his blood.

PEISANDER: Telemachus is an enemy of the people.

HALITHERSES: Your people you mean and a good thing if he is your enemy.

TELEMACHUS: Your people owe my father everything.

DEMOPTOLEMOS: The people owe him nothing but their curses.

POLYBOS: He was a despot, I remember that.

ANTINOUS: Is your outburst at an end, Telemachus? With permission of the chair, I should like briefly to reply to this unwarranted, most unwarranted criticism of those among us who seek the hand of the Queen in marriage. We have just heard from the chair that the claim made by Telemachus, the claim namely that he has some kind of god-given or I don't know what right, to expel us, is invalid. It must be invalid. It is contradicted by laws presented and passed with overwhelming majorities by and in this Assembly. I should not have even bothered to come here today had I known that Telemachus had nothing better to do and no better case to represent than attacking suitors in general and foreigners in particular. It was a pretty unpleasant, one might almost say evil, speech to have to listen to. There is after all a law, and a very sensible law, which forbids anyone in the Assembly to defend tyranny or speak in any way directly or indirectly in favour of tyrants or tyranny.

Never mind that now, Telemachus has committed the damage which he intended to commit and sow suspicion and resentment between Ithacans and non-Ithacans, which presumably was the reason for his wholly unwarranted mention of foreigners.

Citizenship, I should hardly need to mention, plays no role in this issue whatsoever.

The subject is that of marriage to the Queen and who should be allowed to marry her. Good has come out of bad however.

The mask slipped today and we caught a glimpse of what Telemachus really thinks of democracy and republicanism, and that, to put it very mildly, is not much.

AEGYPTIUS: Are you alleging that he was defending tyranny?

POLYBOS: He defended his father. That's defending tyranny.

AEGYPTIUS:	Telemachus, is it true? Were you defending tyranny or is that a calumny intended to discredit your proposal?
TELEMACHUS:	I came here with a petition against the suitors in my father's house.
AGELAUS:	Answer the question!
TELEMACHUS:	A petition. I have a right...
AGELAUS:	Answer the question! Answer the question!
TELEMACHUS:	I was demanding the return of my inheritance.
AGELAUS:	Answer the question!
HALITHERSES:	And what is wrong with that?
ANTINOUS:	He wants more than that.
DEMOPTOLEMOS:	And so do you!
EURYMACHUS:	Allow me: politics is not, or should not, be the issue here, nor the rights or wrongs of the late king's years of rule.
ANTINOUS:	It is relevant. By defending his so-called inheritance rights, Telemachus begins to erect public

places of execution. If we allow him to propagate his ideas like this, he will gnaw away like a rat and the similarly disposed with him, at Ithaca's new freedoms, at the roots of republicanism and the democratic state.

POLYBOS: Telemachus is a revolutionary.

EURYMACHUS: He certainly is not!

POLYBOS: He is more like you than us.

EURYMACHUS: There is no point in starting a slanging match. Telemachus, say concisely what you are requesting. We shall listen.

TELEMACHUS: I have already told you. I want you all to leave.

EURYMACHUS: If that is all, why are you so excited, why is anyone excited? As soon as your mother picks out her future husband from our little group, the unsuccessful hundred and seven will go like lambs.

AGELAUS: Hundred and eight.

EURYAMCHUS: Only if you include the beggar fellow as one of the suitors. (*Laughter*) We are a hundred and seven, not one more.

DEMOPTOLEMOS: Speak for yourselves, I am staying where I am now whatever happens and whoever Penelope marries.

ERYMACHUS: And if you still have trouble with Demoptolemos, we shall all help you to drag him away by his ankles.

DEMOPTOLEMOS: Tyrants everyone of you, that proves it!

EURYMACHUS: You mean we are not anarchists like you. We believe in the rule of law.

ANTINOUS: If you believe in the rule of law, then please listen to me. Do not be misled by the apparent innocence of this man. He has inherited his father's talent to deceive. Just think of his father's trick to capture Troy. This talk of inheritance is if you like, a sort of Trojan horse in the question of inheritance, a way of preparing us to accept the idea of a mystical "right" to do as he pleases. His mother has been learning family tricks too. For years, years now, she fooled us, gullible and trusting as we were, not thinking that a woman could be so underhand, tricking us, with a story of a shroud, an immense shroud she was making for Laertes, her father-in-law. Like all of you, I pitied her and agreed that she had to make no decision before the shroud was ready. She worked three years, three years, on this shroud. She might have gone on weaving an eternal never finished winding sheet if I had not been warned by a little bird that she was undoing during the night what she weaved during the day.

EURYMACHUS: You did not need to bring this story up, Antinous.

ANTINOUS: What Telemachus claims today as his inheritance will be available to the man fortunate enough to marry the widow. Why then waste his time and our time and the time of the entire Assembly, with a petition which has no basis in law? I'll tell you why. He wants you to ignore the law out of pity and by waiving the provisions of the law out of pity, he intends to create a precedent. Pity Telemachus, pity the poor son of a tyrant. There we shall have an anti-democratic precedent for re-establishing the tyranny. That is what the petition is for, disguised as a petition appealing to generous feelings, pity for Telemachus or pity for the poor servants who have so much to do preparing for our feasts.

Make no mistake, our own rights, the rights of free men, would be undermined by accepting this petition. What after all are our democratic rights but rights passed by the general will of all decent people represented in this democratic Assembly? We shall be made to serve the ambitions of the powerful again. Our children will be sent to new wars at the whim of despots because some distant potentate spoke disparagingly of the Ithacan wine. You all know well enough of the appalling sacrifice of war.

HALITHERSES: What sacrifice did you ever make Antinous?

ANTINOUS: Nothing Telemachus has said indicates that we have in any way or at any time in any respect broken any law of Ithaca. He cannot deny that we are fully in our rights to enjoy his hospitality until the day his mother, the widow, reaches a decision and chooses one of us to be her husband.
When she does so, the rest of us will leave at once, without question. Until then we stay, on principle.

AEGYPTIUS: What about the charge that looting has taken place in the palace?

ANTINOUS: Slander.

EURYMACHUS: Not altogether slander, Antinous. What Telemachus meant was that some unruly elements have been wasteful and over-indulgent, and depending upon your point of view, some waste might be described colourfully perhaps, in terms of looting, or shall we say pillage. To some extent I endorse the charge of pillage. It has been so long now since we arrived that some of us, and I name no names, and for sure they represent a tiny minority, have been excessive, extravagant. I am not talking of the majority of suitors, who are responsible and respected men. They abhor, just as Telemachus does, the wasting of good wine and question the number of feasts, which have risen since I arrived at the palace four years ago, from about one a month to one a week. Telemachus and his mother should understand however, that you cannot expect a large group of impatient young men to be timid and patient all the time. The solution, and here of course I do agree with Antinous, lies in the hands of the Queen. She must announce the name of her future husband. It all comes down to time. Time and numbers.

We have waited too long, and yes we are too many. The result of this, and especially over the last year, has been an increasingly unpleasant atmosphere, and that is the last thing I or any sensible person wants to see.

Furthermore, the unpleasant atmosphere, growing feeling of resentment on the one side and impatience on the other side, are being exploited by extremists for their own ends. Some of the suitors have been trying to encourage antagonism between rivals for the Queen. It seems to me that both Antinous and Telemachus are in danger of losing sight of the obvious.

Our problems begin and end with the Queen's decision, or better said, absence of a decision.

As some of you know, Telemachus intends to sail for Sparta shortly, there having been rumours from that place of Odysseus' fate. I understand a journey to Sparta these days will take about a month. Let us give him time to prepare

and leave, arrive in Sparta, make
his enquires, return from Sparta.
Shall we say three months?
At the end of three months then
or when Telemachus returns,
whichever is sooner, the Queen
must decide, I repeat must finally
decide. Further delays take us to a
state of chaos and dissent. If by any
chance, which the heavens forfend,
Telemachus should fail to return,
the Queen shall be made to decide
in any case.

AEGYPTIUS: Are you putting forward an official
proposal?

EURYMACHUS: I am.

AEGYPTIUS: That will require a legal amendment
to the suitors' original right of
residence in the the palace as laid
down in the first legal provision of
their right to stay there.

TELEMACHUS: I object.

AEGYPTIUS: Then you must take your objection
through the appropriate channels.

TELEMACHUS: I thought this Assembly was the
proper channel.

AEGYPTIUS: Objections to new Acts have to go
to the Committee of Public Affairs.

TELEMACHUS: I have never heard of it.

AEGYPTIUS: That is not my fault. Ignorance of the law is no excuse.

DEMOPTOLEMOS: Tyrants do not believe in committees.

TELEMACHUS: What are you talking about? My house, my birthright...

(Chants, catcalls etc.)

TELEMACHUS: My father was a good king to you...

(Voice drowned out by interruptions and catcalls)

EURYMACHUS: Let him speak. He has the right to speak. If we are democrats, we should behave like democrats!

TELEMACHUS: If the suitors are granted the right to live in my home, if my mother can be forced to marry against her will, whose home is safe, what inheritance is safe?
And if we allow the whole of Hellas to propose itself as a suitor for my mother's hand, what is to stop at the boundaries of Hellas? Who is to say that barbarians may not come and ask her for her hand?

(Laughter, catcalls, general hilarity and protests)

ANTINOUS:　　This debate has gone on too long.
　　　　　　Now Telemachus is fantasising.
　　　　　　Barbarians indeed!
　　　　　　I urge, I beg Telemachus to speak
　　　　　　with his mother and prepare her
　　　　　　for her wedding day. Until she
　　　　　　chooses her husband, we all stay
　　　　　　where we are, even Demoptolemos,
　　　　　　if he can bear to continue living
　　　　　　under the same roof as a hundred,
　　　　　　sorry, hundred and seven, would-be
　　　　　　tyrants.
　　　　　　I support and second what
　　　　　　Eurymachus has proposed. Within
　　　　　　three months, the Queen must be
　　　　　　made to take her new husband.

TELEMACHUS:　I'll contest that.

AEGYPTIUS:　　It is your democratic right to do so.
　　　　　　The committee might even
　　　　　　sympathise. For my part I would
　　　　　　say this decision to force the Queen
　　　　　　to marry within a given period of
　　　　　　time is as unconstitutional as the
　　　　　　demand by Telemachus to evict the
　　　　　　suitors from the late king's palace.

ANTINOUS:　　You think so do you!

EURYMACHUS:　*(Aside to Antinous)* Don't be angry.
　　　　　　It isn't worth it. He won't come
　　　　　　back. What Aegyptius said will
　　　　　　actually help us. This looks
　　　　　　thoroughly legitimate.

AEGYPTIUS: Telemachus, is there anything more which you wish to say to the Assembly?

TELEMACHUS: Nothing.

AEGYPTIUS: Has anyone else anything they wish to say?

AEGALUS: It has all been said, now let's put it to the vote!

MENTOR: I have something to say.

ANTINOUS: Mentor! I thought you were dead, old man!

MENTOR: I thought this was the Assembly of Ithaca but I think I must have entered another time or be living in a dream. The insults and disrespect shown to the King and to his son are beyond all measure. Have you forgotten how like a father Odysseus was to you?

AGELAUS. The times have changed. No one thinks like that today. We will have no more kings! Your talk is just reactionary.

EURYMACHUS: (*To Agelaus*) Not here, not now!

MENTOR: There is not one palace which is plundered, but the entire land.

Ithaca is growing sick while the tapeworms of the market grow fat on a land for which they never fought, which they never tend and never loved. The homeland has almost as many immigrants as natives. No one respects the Ithacan customs. The children are hardened and use the lowest language of the streets. The public coffers are plundered by parasites and aliens. Money is made by distortion and usury. Honest work is badly paid. The richest men are middlemen and speculators. The labourer is poor.

Leave the palace if you have any self-respect or shame. If you can show no respect, then I advise you to at least be prudent. Have you not heard rumours? Even the rumours from Sparta tell the same story. Not of a death but of delays. Strange delays. Poseidon the vengeful God blowing the King away from us again and again. Strange temptations and distractions. Weird women that lure sailors to the rocks, out-tricked by Odysseus. The land of forgetfulness, the land called I-have- forgotten-duty, the most dangerous trap of all like a spider's web of idleness and deceit.

Yes, it is said that he was there and somehow escaped. Never do we hear of death, only of delays. There were sailors from Thrace who will swear in a court of law they saw and greeted the King not far from the wild shores of Libya! What would happen if he returned today and found this, his palace full of strangers, suitors drunken and full of meat, the servant girls debauched, the land stripped of wood, and only barren rocks remaining? What will you say when he sees how you have treated his wife, his son, his servants, his land, his country, even his poor dog? Nothing of his sacred to you or beyond the reach of your grasping hands. What if he returns? What if the rumours are true? Then you will run to Poseidon and say "Great God receive us! Hide us!" And better to drown than fall into the hand of this King in anger! I have seen this King in anger.

AGELAUS: We are not afraid of one man and not afraid of two! This is nothing but hate-filled histrionics and wishful thinking!

MENTOR: You have not seen Odysseus angry. You have not seen it! You have not seen him angry!

ANTINOUS:

This proves my warnings! The talk of property rights opens a precedence for all the cranks and prophets of doom to croak their poison! This is the way for the enemies of the republic to gain respectability, with warnings of impending doom.

Mentor, you are wasting time here. Nobody will jump into the sea to save Telemachus a spoilt dinner. Supposing that your prophesy did hold true and we had the pleasant surprise of the unexpected return of Odysseus, he cannot change the law by shaking his spear at us.

We have a right to stay here and a right to vote here and with that right, a few incorrigible reactionaries can do nothing. For the last time, we leave when the Queen decides and not one day before.

MENTOR:

You will not leave even when he stands before you?

EURYMACHUS:

That is not literally what Antinous means. There is no question that we should all leave at once if the King fortuitously returned. You have our assurance of that.

MENTOR:

The king would not need your assurance, Eurymachus.

ANTINOUS: Don't argue with him, there is no point. Mentor, we have a right to stay here, a right, a right! You cannot stop us. Ithaca is a free country.

HALITHERSES: For you lot!

ANTINOUS: Thank the Gods that this indeed a free country. The overwhelming majority of free men find you, Hallisthernes, and your little group of bigoted friends, repugnant and absurd. Repugnant because offensive to decent persons, absurd because he is not coming home, never. I say there will be no return. The old times are finished for ever! There can be no second coming of the king.

MENTOR: I see him! I see him!

AGELAUS: You are mad!

AMPHIMEDON: It is the Ithacan wine which has addled his old brain!

EURYMACHUS: Aegyptius, the vote.

AEGYPTIUS: I call the Assembly to a vote on the motion I read out before.

ANTINOUS: *(To Eurymachus)* What about the other one?

AEGYPTIUS:	What other one? What do you mean?
ANTINOUS:	The motion about the Queen marrying after Telemachus returns from a journey.
AEGYPTIUS:	That will be referred to the committee of Public Affairs..
ANTINOUS:	What is that? I have never heard of it.
EURYMACHUS:	You too Antinous? What is happening to education these days? Get on with your duties, president.
AEGYPTIUS:	I call on the Assembly to vote on the following motion: No suitor be forced to move from the palace of the king unless Telemachus wants him to leave in which case...er, well then he may be.
ANTINOUS:	He has got it all wrong.
EURYMACHUS:	This motion is the formal expression of Telemachus' claim to the right to expel anyone he chooses from his late father's palace. It is a motion which if passed, would thoroughly change the Ithacan laws of residence, giving property owners the right to evict people in their homes.

AMPHIMEDON: It is absolutely anti-democratic.
                People in a home decide if they
                will live there or not.

AEGYPTIUS: Those in favour of the motion.

(Telemachus, Halitherses, and Mentor raise their hands)

AEGYPTIUS: Those against.

(All suitors except Amphinomus raise their hands)

AEGYPTIUS: Those abstaining.

(Amphinomus raises his hand)

AEGYPTIUS: The petition is carried with an
                overwhelming majority. A count
                will not be necessary unless
                Telemachus specifically requests it.
                No? Then I declare this meeting of
                the Assembly of Ithaca hereby
                closed.

(The Assembly breaks up)

ANTINOUS: *(To Telemachus)* What did I tell
                you? You have achieved nothing
                positive. You have simply created
                bitterness.

AMPHIMEDON: *(To Telemachus)* Surprising as it
                may seem to you Telemachus, I love
                Ithaca too. I resent it, I resent it very

much, that you are laying some claim to a monopoly of patriotism. But today we saw your mask slip. You are not a democrat at all. We saw the face of the champion of tyranny.

HALITHERSES: You are making a mistake.

AGELAUS: Yes we are, to allow you in here...

MENTOR: The King is not dead.

AMPHIMEDON: Did you see the King outside a tavern, perhaps you projected that he was coming back upon interpreting the entrails of a pig? Telemachus says his father was not a tyrant, but who is he to judge? He was one of the most evil and despotic people in history and I am glad, yes glad, that he is dead. People were tortured in Ithaca, at your father's command, Telemachus.

AGELAUS: Yes it is true. Even the old man won't deny it. Tell him it is true, old man. Did not the late king advocate torture?

POLYBOS: It is true. Don't try to deny it. There were stonings and crucifixions.

AGELAUS: Not to speak of floggings.

HALITHERSES: He dealt justly. He will deal justly
               when he returns. Melanthius will
               suffer. The day of reckoning...

ANTINOUS: You see? People suffered terribly

DEMOPTOLEMUS: I recall that you were not punished
               for anything, Antinous.

ANTINOUS: As I was only six years old that is
               hardly surprising.

DEMOPTOLEMOS: Just so, you speak as though you
               remember the tyranny. I'd laugh
               if he did come back. I'd laugh to
               see your faces.
               The point I am making is that
               Antinous is being more than a little
               hypocritical with his attack on
               kings. After all, he is an aristocrat
               and dreams of replacing the king,
               not destroying the monarchy.

ANTINOUS: You are an aristocrat too.

DEMOPTOLEMOS: I cannot help the way I was born.
               The difference between you and me,
               Antinous, is that you act like an
               aristocrat, I don't.
               Odysseus and all aristocrats belong
               to the past. There can be no
               exceptions and no new kings.

EURYMACHUS: He is mad.

DEMOPTOLEMOS: And why stop at kings, lawyers too and soldiers and so-called heroes? Let each Ithacan enjoy the fruit of the earth as he needs them and let's have an end to greed and ambition. You talk of rights in the house of Telemachus, but you obviously accept that he has a right to a house just because his father had a house. I say there should be no property and no marriage.

ANTINOUS: Autocrats and anarchists. Ithaca needs neither! Telemachus and Demoptolemos deserve one another. Neither considers the common good.
And this delay is giving them the time they need. I should not be in the least surprised if they plotted together before they came here. Eurymachus is right. If we don't come to a decision about the Queen, the foundations of the state itself will begin to founder.

DEMOPTOLEMOS: Let them founder, let them rot! The men who need the state are men won over to evil. Antinous talks of the old order. Don't imagine that his new order will be more compassionate or more responsible or more just than the thing it has replaced.

He has all the makings of a new Odysseus, this man, all the makings of a tyrant. He is no friend of democracy.

HALITHERSES: All theoretical. The king will return. The day is coming...

AMPHINOMUS: *(Ironically)* Is nigh! Is nigh!

HALITHERSES: Despised and unrecognised he will return to claim his birthright.

AGELAUS: Go back to sleep old man.

PEISANDER: And don't wake up!

EURYMACHUS: It has been years since anyone heard any news from him or about him. He has died at sea, probably in a storm.

POLYBUS: You know what? I think Odysseus's ship was so full of booty ransacked from Troy that his boat sank. *(Laughter)*

AGELAUS: And it was a pity if so you weren't with him, Halitherses.
It is utterly irresponsible for people of your age to upset the young and impressionable. He has been confronted with rapid change and your contribution to the debate was to urge him to hatred and a futile yearning for the past.

(*Exeunt omnes except Amphinomus and Telemachus*)

AMPHINOMUS: Do you really think he is coming back, Telemachus?

TELEMACHUS: I don't know, I don't know. How can I know?

AMPHINOMUS: If he does, remember that I don't drink wine. I don't want...T Telemachus, I think I may go. I'll tell Antinous I have to go. If he comes back, I don't know... Mentor seems so sure. I think if I were you Telemachus, I would feel the same. If your father does come back, remember that I said that...

(*Exit Amphinomus. Telemachus is left on the stage, his head in his hands*)

Act Three Scene One

Sea Shore.
A youth is playing on a flute. Odysseus is lying, motionless.
He cautiously picks himself up. He looks around him. The
youth stops playing.

ODYSSEUS: Where now? Vengeful Poseidon, I can go no further. Torment me no further, Poseidon, there is no need.

YOUTH: No need.

ODYSSEUS: The God of the Waters will never cease tormenting me. He was a friend of Ilios and so he hates me. Well, I am far from Ogygia, that is certain.
This is a time-bound place, a mortal place.
You are not a savage. Believe me, I have been to many places all over the great seas and...you look at me as though you understand, as though you understand Greek.
What a magnificent group of pine! Now as the mists of morning clear I shall better see, better see the place where I have arrived.

YOUTH: Have arrived.

ODYSSEUS: But the goats. There are too many.
              Does the King of this land not see
              there are too many grazing here?
              They root up the saplings of young
              trees. You should tell the King. The
              land will lose its trees.

YOUTH: The King…

ODYSSEUS: Left long ago?

YOUTH: Left long ago.

ODYSSEUS: Have I been here before? At night
              seeing the eyes of the handsome
              lynx. The stream…Is there a
              stream. Is there a stream down
              there…Is there a stream?

YOUTH: There is a stream, running down
              to…

ODYSSEUS: A small cove.

YOUTH: A small cove, yes.

ODYSSEUS: Beyond those rocks and over the
              hill.

YOUTH: The sacred groves…

ODYSSEUS: Sacred to Artemis…

YOUTH: Artemis we have not seen…

ODYSSEUS: The home of the blue thrush and the falcons and the soft breasted doves. What is that noise?

YOUTH: The King's old dog.

ODYSSEUS: Old dog? What king? What king?

YOUTH: Over the brow of the hill there are vineyards.

ODYSSEUS: A God-blessed land!

YOUTH: A God-blessed land? Once God blessed but more than half-forgotten.
Every day more ugly and despoiled. A pillaged land. A violated land. A land that was precious but was neglected. Owners despoil it. They do not care. No sacred groves in their eyes.
The King left us nineteen years ago. I was not born. My mother told me. That dog is old beyond the years of any dog. I took him here. He has waited beyond the years.
There are not so many flies. I expect this is where he used to hunt.
Do you know? Do you…? Are you…? Yes then, oh why…? Why so long? Where were you? Where were you? Where were you?

ODYSSEUS: Argos? Argos? *(Offstage)* Oh, Gods forgive me! Gods forgive me! Gods forgive me! This was too long!

YOUTH: Too long, great king, too long!

ODYSSEUS: *(Returns on stage with corpse of Argos in his arms)* He died as he saw me. He died in my arms but he recognised me. He looked at me and he knew at once who I was. So—I have been recognised. Pallas Athene: did I not say that only if I were recognised, I would stay to fight, but were I not recognised I would return to Poseidon for ever and let not another thought be given to me?

YOUTH: I knew you would return! I never believed what they tell us in classes. Oh joy, oh please dear gods let this not be a dream! Let this not be a dream! Heavenly joy, let this not be, let this not be a mere dream! I could bear anything but that, to wake as though from strong drink and remember dimly a fading hope. Not that, anything but that. Let it not be a dream. That pain would be unbearable. They told me it was impossible and those who said otherwise were just dreamers, fanatics.

ODYSSEUS: Who? What do they tell you?

YOUTH: That you were drowned years ago. I
                   never believed it. Your majesty, I
                   never believed that you had gone
                   for ever.

ODYSSEUS: Great Athene you have held faith.
                   Great Athene! Tell me boy, who
                   rules here? And do you know: how
                   is the Queen? How is my son?

YOUTH: She marries today. She has no
                   choice. Telemachus dares not go to
                   your palace.
                   They tried to murder him as he
                   sailed back from Sparta. He is not
                   far from here.

ODYSSEUS: Who? Who tried to murder him?

YOUTH: Eurymachus and Antinous, two of
                   the most powerful suitors to the
                   Queen.

ODYSSEUS: Where is Telemachus?

YOUTH: He is living in the hut of an old
                   keeper of swine on the other side
                   of the valley.

ODYSSEUS: That will be Eumaeus, faithful as
                   always. What of the goatherd,
                   Melanthius?

YOUTH: First ally and spy to the suitors.

ODYSSEUS: How many of these suitors are in the palace?

YOUTH: Fifty.

ODYSSEUS: Fifty!

YOUTH: Or more. Let me see. I'll number them alphabetically. Agelaus and Amphimedon, he's recent and Amphinomus who is not but shows more courtesy than most of the others. Antinous, their big braggart leader and Ctessipus and the preacher of anarchy, Demoptolemus and Eurydamus and Eurymachus and Eurynomus..

ODYSSEUS: I have been too long! Stop! Stop! Enough!

YOUTH: Leicritus and Leiodes. Leiodes is a priest, of sorts. Peisander of course. We mustn't forget Peisander.

ODYSSEUS: Enough! Oh God, enough!

YOUTH: There are many more. Thoas and Paralus, Agenor.

ODYSSEUS: Insanity!

YOUTH: Hagius, Nichomachus..

ODYXSSEUS: Have you finished?

YOUTH: I have only just begun. Medon,
Agrion, Promus. How many is
that? Oh you know, there must be
more than 50 now. Lestorides,
Agenor, Nisas, er, let me see. Oh
yes, Indius, Minus, Halius, Magnes
and Lyammus, Polydorus, did I
mention him? Perhaps I mentioned
him already. Cynuus, Thriasus,
Pellas, Pronus, Bias and Dulicheus.
Evenorides...

ODYSSEUS: Enough!

YOUTH: Andraemon, Molebus, Promon
or is it Pronomus?

ODYSSEUS: Enough! Enough! Enough!

YOUTH: Elatus, Hippodocus...Phrenius,
Minis...Indius...No wonder with so
many, and I have not named them
all, no wonder that the palace is in a
sorry unkempt state. There are
pools of vomit on the floor. No one
bothers to clear them up now. Your
friends are insulted and worse. They
use your old tapestries for rags.
Everything is filthy. A stench hangs
over all the palace. People are

pouring in from outside Ithaca and
making claims to the land as
though it is theirs.
They claim the palace and your wife
and others claim the fields.

ODYSSEUS: Are these suitors so wealthy that
they can afford to spend all their
days carousing and waiting?

YOUTH: They are wealthy, yes, and will
become more so, not from work
but from speculation and
hoarding and now this of course,
their greatest speculation of all,
their horse race, their betting on
the Queen.

ODYSSEUS: Profiteers fester in the lower rings
of Hades.

YOUTH: All rich men make their wealth
that way today.

ODYSSEUS: I forbade it.

YOUTH: Long ago you forbade it, long ago.
Too long.
Did you think your monuments
could stay for ever if you ignored
them, and if you neglected your
people?
Nineteen years without their king,
the people are turning. Telemachus

told me that they finally brought
her down to the dining hall.

ODYSSEUS: Who?

YOUTH: Your wife. They all announced their
claims to her. Ctessipus offered all
his gold. They say he is the
wealthiest man in Ithaca. He owns
most of the rented property in the
city.
What she said to him was,
"Ctessipus, I would sooner own just
a rag of my absent King than all
your wealth and gold."
Then there was Eurymachus.

ODYSSEUS: Who is Eurymachus?

YOUTH: An advocate, a pleader of forlorn
causes for a profit, a defender of
criminals, a negotiator, a
compromiser, a prevaricator, a
schemer and an agent of deep
destruction.

ODYSSEUS: What did this man called
Eurymachus say?

YOUTH: That he respected the institution of
monarchy. That Penelope should be
entrusted with ruling Ithaca and he
would be her special advisor. To
that she said she could not govern

because her thoughts were fixed
upon you and your return.
Finally Antinous came. He said
that he just wanted her...as a man
wants a woman…that he would
have her..

ODYSSEUS: Enough! Is she unharmed?

YOUTH: Unharmed, you may call it that.
Tonight she must make her final
choice or she may be forced,
forced you understand, by all of
them.

ODYSSEUS: I was too long!

YOUTH: She has long pretended to weave a
shroud, in order to hold them back.
She said she would make a decision
when she had finished weaving it.
By day she wove it. At night she
untied the stitches she made during
the hours of light. They finally saw
how she was tricking them and now
the shroud is finished and the day
of decision has come. The torment
must have an end and a decision
must be reached.

ODYSSEUS: The day of decision.

YOUTH: What will you do? Will you rush to
the place and try and kill as many
as you can?

ODYSSEUS: Before they overwhelm me with
              their numbers? No, I must have a
              strategy. I must be cunning. Help
              me Athene. I must think and act
              with no hesitation but my decision
              must be right. I must have a plan as
              I did then before the walls of Ilios.
              I shall go to them in disguise. I shall
              fool them as we fooled the Trojans.
              I shall go disguised as a beggar. I
              must go in disguise. Will you be
              with me?

YOUTH: I have always been with you.

ODYSSEUS: Find my son. There is no time to
              lose. I must bury the first of the
              faithful.

              (*Exit with corpse of Argos*)

YOUTH: (*Calling*) And there he is!
              Telemachus! Telemachus! There is
              someone here! There is! Why does
              he move so slowly? Faster! Faster!
              Oh trust me! Telemachus! Here!
              Here!

              (*Enter Odysseus*)

ODYSSEUS: Is that my son, over there?

YOUTH: Your son! Your son! Telemachus!
              Telemachus!

ODYSSEUS: Boy? Have you cried out my name?

YOUTH: No.

ODYSSEUS: Let me be the first to tell him.

(Enter Telemachus)

TELEMACHUS: I came as fast as I could. But this
                   man is another beggar. What is
                   more important about him than
                   any other of his kind?

ODYSSEUS: I bring news.

TELEMACHUS: Of my father, I know, I know, more
                   news.

ODYSSEUS: Yes, you seem not very surprised.

TELEMACHUS: Why should I be surprised? I am
                   plagued with false prophets and
                   voices crying: the King! the King! I
                   know what you will be saying,
                   namely that you have seen him
                   somewhere and he is about to
                   return and then you will hold out
                   your hand and ask me to cross it
                   with a coin.
                   Normally I do so to send you on
                   your way and have my peace, but
                   not today. I have no heart for
                   generosity today.

ODYSSEUS: I bring news indeed from your
                   father.

TELEMACHUS: Enough! I have heard this story too many times. Too many times! Heavens, too many times. It is the end.

ODYSSEUS: The end?

TELEMACHUS: The end of hoping and the end of waiting and the end of Ithaca, the end of the island, the end of the land promised us and handed down, all at an end. Today my mother marries a suitor and begets the other race, not the celestial race of beauty but the new race of dirt and gold and growth. They have little time. They will her to bear their children. Even if the stories were true, there is no time left. I did hear from the King of Sparta that there are rumours that he lives, that he has survived as though by miracle every trial placed upon him by the God of the sea and sea change. But play your game then, you have news of course of my father. Is he close?

ODYSSEUS: Closer than you think.

TELEMACHUS: Closer than I think. In my memory he is close enough. I live for memories and what could have been. I have failed him. I have failed my country. It is good that he cannot see this. Ithaca today would break his heart.

ODYSSEUS: The island is still beautiful, despite all that has happened.

TELEMACHUS: If you say so. We mustn't complain. What can any of us do? Our fate is in the hands of the Gods. We are merely their playthings.

ODYSSEUS: Man may be stronger than the Gods!

TELEMACHUS: Stronger than the Gods! I do not think so. My father fought Poseidon and lost. He sank under the mindless waves.
My mother believed that my father would return and claim her. Every day she wove a shroud and took out her stitches in the night.
She thought she could deceive the suitors but it was only delaying fate, it was not stopping fate. We all have to die. We all have to die! All is vanity and futility. Men and women cannot cheat destiny and they cannot cheat death. We fight the tyranny of facts in vain.

ODYSSEUS: Men forge facts, not the Gods of men.

TELEMACHUS: On this day of all days I do not wish
to discuss points of philosophy, old
man.

ODYSSEUS: Listen then. Your father has defied
Poseidon, defied Poseidon and
defeated the oblivion of the sea.
Penelope will be justified. How her
courage shines in my mind's eye in
blatant contrast to your fears and
your whining. I am your father
Telemachus, behave as though you
were proud to be your father's son!

TELEMACHUS: My father is dead!

YOUTH: You wished him so to say so now.
Stand up Telemachus, use the eyes
which fate has given you. Learn to
use your eyes again! To see!

ODYSSEUS: His eyes are dead. He looks at me
with the eyes of someone dead to
the world, weary of combat, weary
of trying to recreate the world.

TELEMACHUS: My father is dead, I say.

ODYSSEUS: Is it proof you need to know I am
your father?

TELEMACHUS: Yes, and a very substantial proof,
not the proof of your word, not
the proof of "I have seen it and
can tell you…"

ODYSSEUS: Did you hear of the boar hunt in the glade below Neritum?

TELEMACHUS: Who did not hear of that? The great hunt, the massive boar.

ODYSSEUS: And your father was hurt.

TELEMACHUS: Yes, he was gored in the left thigh.

YOUTH: It was a deep wound.

TELEMACHUS: He was scarred for life.

ODYSSEUS: Then feel this scar.

YOUTH: The scar.

TELEMACHUS: The scar! (*Telemachus feels the scar.*)

ODYSSEUS. Will you believe me now? Had you no faith? Do you suppose that I would intentionally abandon you? Only my own weakness and folly delayed me but I never wilfully abandoned you, I never consciously willed to abandon you, to deny you, to forget you, I never did.

YOUTH: Weakness and folly.

TELEMACHUS: Oh father! Oh father! Oh God! God! The shame! The shame!

YOUTH: Shame!

ODYSSEUS: My dog waited. He lived beyond the
                 years of any dog to see me. My wife
                 has waited.
                 This poor boy brought up in the
                 fields knew me the moment I
                 arrived. Telemachus, why?

YOUTH: Why?

TELEMACHUS: I was without support. No one
                 believed me.
                 I thought I was mad.
                 They said I was sick and deluded.
                 There was no one I could trust. No
                 one said, come with me, resist this
                 infamy.

ODYSSEUS: Telemachus, for once be honest and
                 tell us.

TELEMACHUS: Father, you cannot imagine.

ODYSSEUS: Be honest.

YOUTH: Honest! Be honest!

TELEMACHUS: I was afraid.

ODYSSEUS: Of death? Of pain? Of punishment?

TELEMACHUS: Yes, yes oh yes, but also of life. I was
                 afraid of life.

ODYSSEUS: For two years I was held captive by
                   a witch. She held me in her power
                   for the same reason.

TELEMACHUS: You? Is that possible?

ODYSSEUS: We always believe the person
                   presented to us. We have not the
                   eyes of Gods to see behind the
                   masks they choose to wear. Yes, I
                   was afraid then of life or at least
                   comfortable with the illusion of
                   contentment which stillness
                   provides. I was afraid to leave her.
                   She made me content and enslaved.
                   I was afraid to face the sea again.
                   The Cyclops had cursed me for
                   blinding him. Poseidon hated me
                   for his blinded son's sake. The
                   friends of Ilios hated me. Like you, I
                   was afraid of drowning. I was afraid
                   of falling into the sea. I overcame
                   myself. I took to the sea again. Yes I
                   was shipwrecked again, but I
                   survived.

TELEMACHUS: Father, it is too late. Surely the boy
                   has told you. It is too late.

ODYSSEUS: Are you my son? I return there
                   tonight. I will avenge this land.

TELEMACHUS: There are more than fifty of them.

ODYSSEUS: So I have been told.

TELEMACHUS: Armed.

ODYSSEUS: So I would expect.

YOUTH: I am going with him Telemachus. Are you not helping us?

TELEMACHUS: You, so young?

YOUTH: So determined yes, and young.

TELEMACHUS: Too young. Against Antinous, against Agelaus? Experienced fighters.

YOUTH: Will you be there to dress my wounds if I am hurt? To avenge me if after all I fall? To bury me and remember me? Will you be there Telemachus, faithful and a comrade?

TELEMACHUS: You would not do so much for me.

YOUTH: Far more, far more.

ODYSSEUS: He looks pale. Even the talk of war makes him tremble. What use is he? Oh you are my shame and punishment, you a son!

YOUTH: Sir, you are wrong. That is not why he is pale.

TELEMACHUS: Do you promise?

YOUTH: On my soul, I promise.

TELEMACHUS: On your soul?

YOUTH: On my soul and its young cage, this body of mine. Learn for once at last to trust, Telemachus son of Odysseus and heir to the throne of Ithaca.

ODYSSEUS: He is afraid. Leave him alone. My son! Shame! Shame! My son afraid, white with terror. He is white I tell you, with fear.

TELEMACHUS: And what if I am? What if I am? Maybe the man white with fear is braver than the man who does not imagine enough to know fear.
I shall fight. I cannot do more than that, father.
I do not need you to tell me about shame. Shame may be overcome, shame may be redeemed, by the act of strength and nobility, by the power of the will.

ODYSSEUS: You have no will to fight and you are afraid to die.

TELEMACHUS: I have a will to love and then I am not afraid to die.

ODYSSEUS: If you had loved Ithaca you would have fought already. You would have done more.

TELEMACHUS: If you had loved Ithaca, you would have returned before! Do not tell me how I failed. Consider your own failings, father. This was too long! You lingered and malingered.

ODYSSEUS: Impertinent boy!

TELEMACHUS: Impertinent for telling the truth. I am not afraid now.

ODYSSEUS: But you do not fight for honour, for your country.

TELEMACHUS: Honour and country mean everything to me now but do not question me about the way to them. It is the privilege of every man to choose his own way to redemption.

ODYSSEUS: Words, philosophy! Excuses for prevarication. If you have found your courage, then prove it to me Telemachus.

TELEMACHUS: Try me then.

ODYSSEUS: Go now to the palace if you have the courage to do so. Not secretly, no. Make sure your arrival is well

advertised. Make the biggest fanfare
of it that you can. They will not dare
kill you in front of the masses.
Besides, they have the marriage on
their minds. Let their greed be their
undoing. Tell them you have come
to preside over the festivities and
see your mother married.
The disappointing trip to Sparta
has convinced you of the futility of
further resistance.
The shroud is finished. That is what
you will say. The shroud is finished.
The shroud is finished.

YOUTH: The shroud is finished!

TELEMACHUS: The shroud is finished.

ODYSSEUS: Take charge of the preparations. I
                think they will grant that. Insist on
                it. They will see it as a humiliation
                and an acknowledgement of their
                new order.

YOUTH: Their new order.

ODYSSEUS: Remove the weapons from the
                banqueting hall. Leave just three
                spears and three shields.

TELEMACHUS: What if someone sees me and
                asks me why?

ODYSSEUS: Then you say that a few weapons you are leaving for security but removing most because the smoke will tarnish the iron. Use your authority. Who may be trusted there?

TELEMACHUS: Eurycles, Phemius, Mento, Halitherses. No one else.

ODYSSEUS: You mean all the rest, our entire household, has gone over to them?

TELEMACHUS: You were too long!

YOUTH: Too long!

ODYSSEUS: I know, heavenly Gods, I know!

TELEMACHUS: Too long, we waited too long. You said you would return. We thought you meant in months or a year, not years, not nineteen years. Melanthius, the keeper of the goats, has shown them where to find the best of everything. The serving maids are whores to the invader, all but two of them.

ODYSSEUS: The whores will be hacked in pieces and fed to the swine. Melanthius will find a traitor's end. Too long! Too long! Heavenly Gods, too long!

YOUTH: Revenge in time, now you must act!

ODYSSEUS: When I arrive I shall do so as a beggar. Can you arrange to have me admitted and this boy admitted?

TELEMACHUS: It should not be difficult. They are generous with your wealth. Tonight of all nights they will want to see the world witness to the collapse of the old order and the downfall of the Queen of Ithaca.

ODYSSEUS: Is there anything the youth can bring them which will make them favour him?

TELEMACHUS: Eumaeus has kept the best swine hidden from them. I know where. We can take one of those. The youth can say he found them in a special sty and has brought it for the slaughter.

ODYSSEUS: Good. We shall all act at once on a signal. They will have no weapons. We shall take the three swords before they know what is happening. If Telemachus and I keep looking at one another they may become suspicious. There must be a clear signal.

YOUTH: When I say strike you will strike. Trust me.

ODYSSEUS: Then we shall trust you.
             Telemachus, the Queen must stay
             indoors until the work is finished.

(Exit Telemachus)

ODYSSEUS: Who are you? You gave him
             strength. I could not reach him.

YOUTH: Your shadow, Odysseus.

ODYSSEUS: My shadow, what nonsense,
             nevertheless, you seem to have
             worked on him. What did you say
             which made him different? He was
             so afraid at first, he was paralysed
             with fear.

YOUTH: Phemius sang of war, of eternal war
             and love. That must be enough for
             you. To know, I mean, that love and
             war are brother and sister, and
             always have been.
             Question anything, Odysseus but
             love. Love may not be questioned.
             Aphrodite and her son may never
             be questioned. That is the way of
             blasphemy and the path to
             desolation.
             Where there is love, there must be
             veneration.
             Odysseus, the trickster, you are
             sometimes too much the strategist
             and the inquisitor. Simply be happy
             that you have found your son again.

ODYSSEUS: Yes, we have all found ourselves
                 again today.

YOUTH: The shroud is finished and Ithaca
                 has found herself again.

                 (Exeunt)

Act Three Scene Two

The great banqueting hall of Ithaca. Servants are preparing for a feast.

All the suitors.

ANTINOUS: Let her have her last wishes on the last day of her widowhood. We can afford to be generous. Tomorrow she will have a husband. The shroud is finished.

DEMOPTOLEMOS: It is not fair, Antinous. You agreed to this plan because you know it does not give the weaker and older suitors a chance.
How can most of us be expected to pull a bow as huge as the late king's? You and the Queen arranged this in advance.
It is a conspiracy. It is you she wants to marry and to save face and to give the appearance of some sort of equal chance, you engineer this competition, but the results have been planned in advance. This is the subterfuge of princes against the people.

ANTINOUS: I resent that implication.

AGELAUS: The competition is not pointless. You speak like that because you are puny. I am as strong as Antinous.

EURYMACHUS: It is the Queen's last request. Antinous was generous and shrewd in granting her this wish. The people will recognise a noble gesture.

DEMOPTOLEMOS: Eurymachus, we are not in the business of making noble gestures; at least we should not be in such a business. We are here as suitors, some of us at least. There are other considerations apart from the ability of her next husband to pull a bow. We must think of what will be the most just and equal government.
What the people have invested in is not to know who can or cannot pull an instrument of war.

ANTINOUS: In what, according to you, have the people invested?

DEMOPTOLEMOS: Fair and democratic government for Ithaca. That is the demand of the people. Democracy. They do not care who can pull some bow longest. Ctessipus agrees with me.

ANTINOUS: I am sure he does.

DEMOPTOLEMOS: It is what I have always maintained. Antinous is ambitious. He will be king. We replace one tyrant with another.

ANTINOUS: Yes, I am ambitious. Since when was ambition a crime? I want that woman. I am ambitious for her. I shall not let the whining of those less successful than I stand in my way.

DEMOPTOLEMOS: If Telemachus had spoken like that in the Assembly you would have said that he was attacking democracy. Your attacks on the late tyrant are a sham, a sham because you intend to replace him. You are an aristocrat. Yes, yes and so am I. The difference is that you act like one. Odysseus belongs to the discards of history and so do you! And lawyers and soldiers and peasants and heroes, architects and writers.
Let them all perish. Let each Ithacan enjoy the fruits of the earth as he needs them. You still talk of "rights" to the palace of Telemachus, which is as much as to say you believe in property rights and the rights to have a wife. I say away with property! Away with marriage!

EURYMACHUS: He is mad!

ANTINOUS: Anarchists and autocrats! Ithaca
                needs neither. Telemachus and
                Demoptolemos deserve each other.
                This delay has given them
                opportunities. I should not be
                surprised if they agreed to these
                protests together. They both want
                continued delay.
                Eurymachus is right. Allowing the
                Queen to keep us waiting with this
                ludicrous story of the shroud was a
                great mistake. Well, the shroud is
                finished and the time has come.

DEMOPTOLEMOS: Antinous, you are no friend of
                democracy.

ANTNIOUS: Really, Demoptolemos, do you not
                find this competition democratic?
                Anyone may enter, even you.

AMPHINOMUS: Perhaps we should consider...

ANTNIOUS: Consider?

AMPHINOMUS: Consider what Telemachus thinks.

ANTINOUS: I have considered.

DEMOPTOLEMOS: Antinous considered.
                Votes are not necessary for
                Antinous.

ANTINOUS: There has been enough considering my friend. Today is the day of decision. The shroud is finished.

AMPHINOMUS: But if we consider…

ANTINOUS: No more considering! The shroud is finished!

EURYMACHUS: Calm my friend, calm!

DEMOPTOLEMOS: We took no vote on this competition of yours Antinous. Are you sure a majority would favour it?

AMPHINOMUS: This competition makes me uneasy.

DEMOPTOLEMOS: You are right to feel uneasy. It is a trick invented by Antinous to ensure he wins the widow and obtains complete power.

AGELAUS: Amphinomus, another whining weakling!

AMPHINOMUS: You misunderstand me. It is something else. Surely you have heard what they say about that bow.

AGELAUS: Who say? Say what?

AMPHINOMUS: Telemachus says that only his father can pull that bow.

ANTINOUS: And that frightens you? Awww!

AMPHINOMUS: It is a provocation to the Gods to
                   challenge such a legend. It is
                   tempting Fate to proclaim that the
                   man who can draw the bow and
                   shoot an arrow furthest is husband
                   to the Queen.
                   It seems like an invitation to the
                   King to be present.

ANTINOUS: Now that is a mute point. Are
                   ghosts eligible to participate? We'll
                   need to ask Eurymachus for his
                   professional opinion on that. Are
                   ghosts allowed to enter such
                   competitions? Ha! Ha!
                   Seriously, how can intelligent men
                   listen to such old wives' tales?
                   Or is this perhaps a ruse you and
                   Demoptolemos have concocted to
                   defer a decision again, so you can
                   continue to live in the palace and...

DEMOPTOLEMOS: And you cannot replace the tyrant!

AGELAUS: Do not be so sure that you will win,
                   Antinous.

ANTINOUS: If you are my strongest opponent,
                   Agelaus, then I am sure.

*(In the background, Youth has entered quietly and is
removing weapons)*

EURYMACHUS: Heh you! Stop that! What do you think you are doing?

YOUTH: I am removing the weapons.

AGELAUS: We can see that.

ANTINOUS: Why are you removing the weapons? Who are you anyway?

(Enter Telemachus)

TELEMACHUS: He is acting on my orders, Antinous. He answers to me.

EURYMACHUS: Telemachus! What a delightful surprise! How delightful to see you home again.

ANTINOUS: The three months is passed.

TELEMACHUS: I know what is happening.

EURYMACHUS: But tell us about your trip. Was there news?

ANTNIOUS: You have made yourself smart I see and have arrived back in time to assist at our festivities and see who is to become your happy father-in-law.

TELEMACHUS: Yes, I have brought news of my father. I narrowly escaped drowning on my return from Sparta.

ANTINOUS: Unlike your father. So we heard. So
               we heard.

EURYMACHUS: Very interesting! You can tell us all
               about it at the feast tonight.

TELEMACHUS: We were pursued by pirates shortly
               after leaving the harbour.

AMPHINOMUS: Pirates! I thought there were no
               pirates in the waters around
               Sparta.

EURYMACHUS: You can never tell these days. We
               live in troubled times.

TELEMACHUS: Yes, in anxious times. It was as
               though they had been waiting for us
               and expecting us. Their ships were
               drawn on either side of us, shortly
               after the exit from the port. That
               way the wind could not blow
               against all of them.

EURYMACHUS: But how wonderful that you have
               managed to arrive home tonight of
               all nights.

TELEMACHUS: Yes, the shroud is finished.

EURYMACHUS: The shroud is finished. The Queen...

TELEMACHUS: Has a husband.

ANTINOUS: Who is the boy?

TELEMACHUS: A shepherd boy. He has brought you a new pig.

ANTINOUS: A shepherd boy and he brings a pig. Ha! Ha! A surprising feat.

YOUTH: I know where fine pigs are kept. I have brought a pig from Eumaeus.

ANTINOUS: Excellent. We shall have a sacrificial pig when Penelope has found her husband. But what is the sense of clearing the hall of weapons?

DEMOPTOLEMOS: Antinous thrills to the sight of weapons. They make him feel powerful, like a man, like a King.

TELEMACHUS: The iron will be tarnished by the smoke. We shall keep a few arms as elementary security but we hardly expect an army to attack us tonight.

ANTINOUS: Very well. Do not let strangers into these halls without warning us in future. You will frighten Amphinomus out of his skin.

(Enter more suitors and Irus, a beggar and Odysseus in the disguise of a beggar)

IRUS: Someone is in my place!

ODYSSEUS: Leave me be. I am here today.

IRUS: My lords! This is not fair. I have always been the beggar here. What right has this man to usurp my place?

AEGELAUS: This will be a laugh. Let's see if they fight. Irus, don't stand for it.

ODYSSEUS: I have no quarrel with you. This was never your place.

IRUS: Never my place? It has always been my place, as long as anyone can remember. I came here. I have been here for years. Never my place! Who are you more like, coming in here and thinking you have a right to be here.

ANTINOUS: Stranger, you have taken his place.

ODYSSEUS: For one day we can share the scraps. Tomorrow I shall give you satisfaction.

IRUS: Give me satisfaction? What kind of language is that? I would sooner have satisfaction now. What right have you to be here?

ODYSSEUS: I shall not be here long.

IRUS: You are right about that! You will not be in my place long! With your permission, lords, he should be whipped.

ODYSSEUS: All that you lose today will be repaid tomorrow.

IRUS: You will repay what I lose will you? Get out now.

ANTINOUS: Let's have him whipped now. It will be a diversion before the meal begins. We can listen to his songs of pain as the leather cracks his pallid skin.

EURYMACHUS: I have a better idea: let the two beggars fight it out between them.

ANTINOUS: Let the two beggars fight! Excellent idea.

ODYSSEUS: I say I have no quarrel with this man. Then I shall beg no scraps today.

IRUS: Now he says he will beg no scraps. No stomach for a whipping or a fight. Well, that's not enough. You must lick my feet and say, "Great lord Irus, pardon me."

(Laughter)

TELEMACHUS: *(Aside)* How much longer? How much longer?

YOUTH: *(Aside)* Not yet, not yet.

ANTINOUS: Make a ring, see them fight.

IRUS: Will you turn the other cheek? Turn the other cheek? *(Kicks Odysseus. General laughter.)*

AGELAUS: Now the other one is becoming angry. Look at his face!

ANTINOUS: Irus, the scrounger who loses this fight will be whipped till he has no skin left on his back.

AGELAUS: And he will lose his precious place too.

IRUS: Then we can throw this beggar onto the heap where that dog is.

YOUTH: *(Aside to To Telemachus)* Not yet! Not yet!

ODYSSEUS: The dog that belonged to the late King?

ANTINOUS: It may have been the king's. What is that to you? We got bored with feeding it scraps.

AGELAUS: And besides, it depressed us with its graveyard looks and whimpering and howling for its late master.

ANTINOUS: Irus entertains us better than a stupid dog.

IRUS:	I held it back and Melanthius kicked the stupid cur hard and long between the legs.
	Then it stopped howling so much. Instead of a deep growling dog, it sounded more like a squeaky cat after that. It changed from going bow wow to meow! Meow! Ha! Ha!
	(Irus begins to speak more hesitantly as he sees Odysseus discard his rags and he sees how strong Odysseus appears.)
	Anyway, say you are sorry and we'll forget the fight.
EURYMACHUS:	Too late, Irus!
AGELAUS:	Irus, you coward.
ANTINOUS:	This new beggar looks quite strong. He may beat Irus after all.
IRUS:	It is all right, we don't need to fight. I let him off.
AGELAUS:	You should have thought of that before. It is too late to back down now, Irus.
ANTINOUS:	And a whipping Irus, remember?

(Odysseus and Irus fight. In a few moments Odysseus has knocked Irus senseless. Irus tries to raise himself, groans and falls back on the ground. Much laughter from the suitors)

ANTINOUS: Throw him outside, where the dog
              used to be but we had better spare
              him the whipping. He would die.
              Stranger, that was good
              entertainment.

ODYSSEUS: I am not here for your
              entertainment, Antinous.

ANTINOUS: (*Strikes him*) Nobody talks to me
              like that!

TELEMACHUS: Antinous, I expect even beggars to
              be treated with respect within these
              walls.

ANTINOUS: Even beggars. Even beggars.
              (*Takes Odysseus's tunic to wipe
              table.*) Oh I am sorry! I thought this
              was a rag. (*Laughter.*)

AMPHINOMUS: Antinous, leave the beggar.

ANTINOUS: Seen another vision have we,
              Amphinomous? Has Pallas Athene
              turned into a swallow and dropped
              her little message on your head?
              (*Laughter.*)

AMPHINOMUS: Antinous, this is his father's house.

ANTINOUS: His father's? Well sure. I did not
              think it was his mother's did I?
              (*Laughter.*)

ODYSSEUS: (*Aside*) Patience, Pallas Athene give me patience. Your permission, kind sirs, to beg for alms?

AGELAUS: Let him Antinous. It is policy to treat beggars well. Sometimes the Gods disguise themselves as beggars in order to test us.

ANTINOUS: There is too much superstition in Ithaca. I thought you at least were free of it.

AGELAUS: It is not superstition, but policy. You never know what friends you might need.

ODYSSEUS: Sir, give only what you wish to freely give. If you have a guilty conscience, you cannot buy your pardon with another man's wealth.

(Odysseus goes from suitor to suitor begging for scraps of food, which he places in a pouch which he is carrying)

DEMOPTOLEMOS: Why is the Queen not here?

TELEMACHUS: I told her to wait in her rooms.

DEMOPTOLEMOS: Why?

EURYMACHUS: Does it matter? Besides, Telemachus is right. This would be no sight for a woman.

ODYSSEUS: *(To Amphinomous)* Thank you sir. Will you take advice from a man who has seen much?

AMPHINOMUS: What advice can you give me, old man?

ODYSSEUS: Leave this place now. These men are doomed. You show some signs of a guilty conscience. That is already much. These men insult our Gods. They will all die today.

AMPHINOMUS: I understand you. You are only a beggar and you are shocked. Do not fret old man, this is the last night.

ODYSSEUS: Yes, it is the last night of shame.

EURYMACHUS: I heard that beggar man. If you think you are being funny, you would do well to learn a new kind of humour.

ODYSSEUS: Are you the shrewd and cunning lawyer they call Eurymachus?

EURYMACHUS: Perhaps, and what is that to you?

ANTINOUS: Old man, we have given you the opportunity to take your place in the corner and we have allowed you the right to beg for food. Be satisfied with that.

POLYBOS: Beggars! Give them an inch and
                    they will take a mile!

AGELAUS: Don't come near me, parasite!

AMPHINOMUS: Agelaus, it is not customary to
                    refuse hospitality to a beggar.

AGELAUS: I know, I know, they may be
                    ambassadors of the Gods. Well, if it
                    makes you feel better. *(Gives some
                    food to Odysseus.)*

ANTINOUS: You can say what you like,
                    Amphinomus, I am not giving
                    anything to this old man.

ODYSSEUS: What you have to give is not yours.

ANTINOUS: I'll give you something then that
                    certainly is mine. Come here.

*(Odysseus goes to him. Antinous hits him with great
strength in the face. Odysseus withstands the blow without
staggering)*

YOUTH: *(Aside)* Not yet, not yet.

ANTINOUS: Still awaiting a sign from Pallas
                    Athene anyone?

ODYSSEUS: You are young and in the best of
                    health, but sometimes the work is
                    finished when we least expect it to

end. Irus was proud and full of
expectation and now he is finished.
Be grateful for what you had.

ANTINOUS: Old man, only the importance and
joyfulness of this occasion prevents
me from having you put to death.

AMPHINOMUS: The old man did not flinch. A
beggar fed all his life on scraps
could not have stood up to such a
blow.

ANTINOUS: This is too much. Take this idiot
away before I kill him.

EURYMACHUS: Wait. I have an idea. This old man
obviously thinks he is a prophet.
You should not talk like that to an
emissary of the Gods, Antinous.
(Laughter.) No doubt you were
once a king old man? And owned a
palace much like this one?
(Laughter.)

ODYSSEUS: I have travelled miles from my
kingdom. I have seen terrible
things.

EURYMACHUS: The sight of his wife!

AGELAUS: Or the meals she makes for him!

EURYMACHUS: Do you have a wife?

ODYSSEUS: I have a wife.

EURYMACHUS: Is she maintained by you in the style to which she is accustomed?

ANTINOUS: Demoptolemos, you have fallen very silent. What is it? Do you not care for this representative of the people? I notice that you did not give him very much from your plate. I thought you believed in equality. What is the matter? Is this beggar not someone with whom you can share all of your wealth? Here is a golden opportunity to show us the meaning of comradeship and communism. Show us by example. Should he not also have the right to apply for the hand of the Queen? According to you that is what democracy is all about, the rule of the People... Is that not right?

EURYMACHUS: Antinous, you take the joke too far.

DEMOPTOLEMOS: Antinous is joking but I am not when I say, of course if this beggar wishes to take part in the competition he may do so. In a true democracy he would be entitled.

ANTINOUS: There you are everybody, that's what I said. That is democracy, as understood by our friend here, although I notice he has avoided the question of redistribution of his own wealth.

DEMOPTOLEMOS: Women should be allowed to choose their own husbands, men should not choose for them.

EURYMACHUS: Do you agree with that old man?

ODYSSEUS: I do agree, with the provision that the woman knows how to choose a man.

EURYMACHUS: And how should a woman know how to choose a man, on what basis? Women can be very erratic in their choice sometimes.

ODYSSEUS: The woman must be fit to bear his children.

DEMOPTOLEMOS: Fit to bear his children! What elitist folly!

ODYSSEUS: The woman judges a man by the children she can bear. No woman should be forced to marry a man unworthy of her.

DEMOPTOLEMOS: More elitism.

EURYMACHUS: I agree with the beggar man.

CTESSIPUS: So do I. I shall take nothing from the Queen if I marry her.

AGELAUS: But you won't give her anything either! (*Laughter.*)

ANTINOUS: Old man, you will take part in our competition. We are holding a competition this evening and you may take part if you wish. Boy, make yourself useful, get the hoops ready, set up a row of them from here to the far door there...
              (*Youth begins setting up hoops*).
              By special request of the Queen herself, her final decision as to who her future husband will be is to be decided by which man shows the greatest dexterity in stringing and shooting arrows from a bow through the hoops which will be now put up at the end of the hall. It will be quite a task to shoot an arrow through all the hoops.

AMPHINOMUS: Antinous, do not ask the beggar to take part in this.

ANTINOUS: Why ever not?

EURYMACHUS: Amphinomus is right. It is a joke in poor taste.

ANTINOUS: But it is not a joke. I want to see the beggar perform better than

Demoptolemos. I think he can but I doubt that either of them can even string the bow. It will be hugely entertaining to watch them try.

EURYMACHUS: I do not see the point. It will create a bad precedent.

POLYBOS: My son, you should show more respect to Antinous. You are the man creating a bad precedent by not deferring to your social superior.

EURYMACHUS: And what of the respect due to the Queen by allowing beggars to take part in this competition? Have you thought of that?

ANTINOUS: I shall decide what is and what is not respectful towards the Queen.

EURYMACHUS: Telemachus, will you allow this beggar to take part in the competition?

TELEMACHUS: If he agrees, he may.

ANTINOUS: So beggar man, you have heard. Do you agree? Will you take part in our competition?
Fetch the bow, Telemachus.

(Exit Telemachus)

ODYSSEUS: It will be an honour for me to take
                 part. Perhaps this evening I shall
                 have the opportunity to make good
                 some of the wrongs which I have
                 done to my poor wife.

ANTINOUS: Would your wife be pleased to
                 know you are here?

ODYSSEUS: There is no place I think, where she
                 would sooner see me.

ANTINOUS: You will be able to go home to her
                 and proclaim to her—wife! I took
                 part in a competition and, well
                 come to think of it, as you are
                 married you had better not tell her
                 what the competition was about!

EURYMACHUS: Exactly—the beggar is married,
                 that must disqualify him anyway.

ODYSSEUS: If I should win this competition, I
                 shall take no second wife.

ANTINOUS: How reassuring. *(Laughter.)* The
                 strange boy will be our judge.

YOUTH: Your Judge! When I give the signal,
                 the shooting can begin.

ANTINOUS: Excellent! We have a strange boy to
                 judge us. So much for etiquette.

YOUTH: To judge you.

EURYMACHUS: I am not taking part.

DEMOPTOLEMOS: Neither am I and I protest against the elitist nature of this entire competition.

ANTINOUS: Well, doesn't that just give the rest of us a better chance now that you heroes have opted out? What about you Agelaus, are you afraid as well?

AGELAUS: I am not afraid of you, Antinous.

(Telemachus brings bow)

ANTINOUS: I am glad of that, Agelaus. I always hoped we could treat one another with mutual respect.

TELEMACHUS: The bow has been kept in good condition but nobody has tried to use it since my father left, nineteen years ago. They say that nobody save he could use it.

ANTINOUS: Who are "they"?

TELEMACHUS: My father said so. My mother told me the story.

ANTINOUS: And the Queen is hoping that no one will be able to pull this bow.

If either you, Telemachus, or your mother are hoping this could be another delaying tactic, think again. Whatever happens, she will still have to take a husband. There will be no more delays. The shroud is finished. If we have to, because nobody can string the bow, that will not give you the chance for another delay, we shall gather round a table and hammer out an agreement. Even if we have to shut ourselves in a room with no food, we shall reach a decision. The shroud is finished and the time has come…Do you understand?

Now, Ctessipus, show us how it is done.

CTESSIPUS: (*Tries unsuccessfully to string bow*) The trouble is that I have rheumatism these days. In the joints of my fingers…No, it is no use…Someone younger had better try.

ANTINOUS: Polybos.

POLYBOS: There is no point. It is true what he says. Someone younger should try.

ANTINOUS: As you wish. Eurymachus?

EURYMACHUS: I have already said that I am not participating.

DEMOPTOLEMOS: Antinous is only asking us first to make his own efforts seem more impressive.

EURYMACHUS: Agelaus may beat him.

AMPHIMEDON I'll try. It cannot be so difficult, Ctessipus. *(Tries and fails)*. It does not work. There is something wrong with it.

EURYMACHUS: Admit it. You are not as strong as Antinous.

DEMOPTOLEMOS: That's what he wants you all to say.

AMPHIMEDON: I should be amazed if he could string it. No one could. It is not normal.

ANTINOUS: Amphinomus, are you ill? Amphinomus, why don't you answer?

AMPHIMEDON: He's sulking.

ANTINOUS: No doubt he has seen another omen. Agelaus, you try.

AGELAUS: The bow needs greasing.
(Tries without success).
It's hopeless. No, it can't be done, can't be done. The string has been strung too tightly, that's what it is, or something has happened to it

over the years. Well that's that then. *(Flings down bow in disgust.)*

ANTINOUS: So, we shall see. *(Antinous picks up the bow. He makes every effort to string it but he fails. After many efforts, he gives it up and throws the bow down.)* I cannot do it. So we cannot do it. Probably the last king could not either. I never saw him use it. This is some kind of trick. And it is obvious now why the widow wanted this competition. She knew it was impossible to string and saw the chance for a new delaying tactic, especially if people believed in the silly myths about it. As I have said, that will not work. She will have a husband tonight. The shroud is finished and the time has come for her to choose. Bow or no bow, and by whatever means necessary she will have her husband tonight.

TELEMACHUS: You are forgetting someone, Antinous.

ANTNIOUS: Forgetting someone?

TELEMACHUS: A competitor.

ANTINOUS: A comp...? Oh, don't tell me you want to enter this competition, Telemachus.

AMPHIMEDON   For his mother! (*Laughter*)

TELEMACHUS: You said the old man may try.

ODYSSEUS: Yes, I should like to see for myself if this bow is as useless or as hard to string as everybody claims.

ANTINOUS: Very well, I shall go down to talk to that youth at the end and there are maybe other persons here who want to try before I do. This old man depresses me.

AMPHIMEDON: Isn't that dangerous? You would be directly in the old man's line of fire.

ANTINOUS: Dangerous? Danger from the beggar? I think not. Boy, we must be boring you. (*Moves down off stage.*)

ODYSSEUS: Pallas Athene, do not fail me now. (*Strings the bow with ease, fits an arrow, takes aim.*)

EURYMACHUS: Antinous! Be careful! The beggar has strung the bow! The beggar has strung the bow!

ANTINOUS: I shall be careful. I'm supposed to be marrying soon. This is my stag night.

YOUTH: (*Voice off-stage*) The Gods be with
the Right! Shoot sir, shoot!

TELEMACHUS: The signal!

ODYSSEUS: Pallas Athene has answered my call.
The shroud is finished! (*Fires
arrow.*)

YOUTH: (*Voice off-stage*) The old man wins!
The old man wins!
(*Enters dragging body of Antinous.*)
A direct hit through both ears.
A perfect shot. He wins.

(*During the confusion, horror and disbelief which ensues,
Telemachus takes down the weapons from the walls*)

AGELAUS: That unlucky lucky shot was your
last, old man.

(*Telemachus throws arms to Youth and to Odysseus*)

ODYSSEUS: Do you not recognise me? Your
King, returned from shattered Ilios,
guided by the Fates.

DEMOPTOLEMOS: The tyrant has returned!

ODYSSEUS: Your rightful king is returned. I was
too long, too long but now I am
returned. I bring you the thunder of
the wrath of the Gods and the fury
of divine destruction. The shroud is
finished and the King has returned
to Ithaca.

POLYBOS: The tyrant perished in the ocean.
              You have no proofs. You are another
              fraud.

ODYSSEUS: Proofs? Once more you want
              proofs? I who alone could string the
              bow of kings. I bear the scar. Do
              you recognise this scar? *(Shows
              Polybos the scar.)*

TELEMACHUS: What is the matter, Polybos? Have
              you seen a ghost?

POLYBOS: The scar! The King got that scar
              twenty-two years ago. I would
              recognise it anywhere. This man is
              Odysseus.

EURYMACHUS: Great King! Welcome back to
              Ithaca! You have dealt justly.
              Antinous was ambitious and
              unscrupulous. He ignored my
              advice. He was plotting to take over
              in Ithaca and set up a tyranny. I was
              always trying to warn him that you
              might not be dead, that we could
              not be sure, but he would not listen.
              I always tried to defend your son
              and the Queen against his insults.
              Telemachus, tell him it is true. He
              can't deny it. Tell him, Telemachus.

ODYSSEUS: My palace has been turned into a
              whore house.

EURYMACHUS: Blame Amphimedon for that. I
              always tried to keep some kind of
              order and restrain people. I said the
              women must show restraint.

ODYSSEUS: My wine was emptied over the
              floors.

EURYMACHUS: Blame Amphimedon for that. I am
              not at all a heavy drinker.

ODYSSEUS: My wife was insulted.

EURYMACHUS: But never by me. I once told
              Ctessipus to show more respect.

ODYSSEUS: They threw my dog on a dunghill.

EURYMACHUS: Yes, yes, I understand. And you
              have other just causes for
              complaint. When all is said and
              done, you have good reason to be
              quite dissatisfied with the way
              affairs have been conducted during
              your long absence.
              I therefore would like to make a
              proposal. That every suitor pays you
              with an appropriate appreciation,
              shall we say twelve percent interest,
              on the value of everything which
              has been consumed here during
              your long absence in addition of
              course to the replacement of what
              has been lost.

And a special supplement to be paid by those who actually lodged here. Now that is fair isn't it? Surely that is fair? You cannot ask for more. Twelve percent interest. That is fair.

TELEMACHUS: This is fair! (*Telemachus runs his sword through Eurymachus and then hacks him down*)

EURYMACHUS: Where am I going to? Oh mercy, dark night. (*Dies.*)

AMPHINOMOUS. The door!

DEMOPTOLEMOS: I can't open it. It is locked from the outside!

(*Agelaus appears with arms for the suitors*)

YOUTH: Melanthius must be giving them arms from the cellar.

ODYSSEUS: Go and find out!

(*Exit youth*)

AGELAUS: What are we afraid of? We outnumber the tyrants. There is no point in cowering in the corner, you cowards. He will show you no mercy because you did not fight. If we stand as one together we can defeat them.

(Fighting ensues. Only a few suitors such as Agelaus and Demoptolemos show courage. The suitors are killed. Enter Youth)

YOUTH:　　　　　　It is what I thought. Melanthius had been raiding the cellar for arms. I jumped on him tied him up and strung him up to the rafters. Telemachus, you are wounded.

TELEMACHUS:　　　A scratch. Look out!

(Demoptolemos, who seemed to be dead, revives, tries to kill youth from behind. Telemachus kills him. Massacre of remaining suitors follows. Cries for mercy are ignored)

ODYSSEUS:　　　　Are they all dead? Is the shame dead?

YOUTH:　　　　　　Dead, yes, dead. The shame is dead.

ODYSSEUS:　　　　Are any apart from the women still living?

(Phemius emerges from hiding and grasps his legs)

PHEMIUS:　　　　　Spare me King.

ODYSSEUS:　　　　What are you?

PHEMIUS:　　　　　The provider of music to these halls.

ODYSSEUS:　　　　Why should I spare your life if you played for them?

TELEMACHUS: He played for them because he had to. Now he will play for us.

ODYSSEUS: No, he must pay with his blood too. He played for them.

YOUTH: Proud man, will you sink in blood?

TELEMACHUS: I need his songs.

YOUTH: The shroud is completed. It is enough. Do not recreate the horrors.

ODYSSEUS: Another demon! Let him die.

YOUTH: Fight too long with demons and become a demon. Use him as your messenger. He has a strong voice.

ODYSSEUS: Very well, go to the people. *(Phemius rushes out. Odysseus shouts after him)* Tell them the years of misrule are over. The shroud is completed. The King has returned. The days of shame are ended.

YOUTH: Telemachus, let me tend this wound. It is a deep cut. There are splinters of iron under the skin.

ODYSSEUS: Go the women. Divide them into two groups. Those who remained loyal remain behind. The others remove the bodies, clean the floors, perfume the air. Then they will be hanged, the whores.

YOUTH: Whores. Whores.

ODYSSEUS: I know what a whore is, youth.

YOUTH: What is a whore?

ODYSSEUS: The woman who sells herself for gain.

YOUTH: Yes, but understand these were real whores, not those who gave excitedly of their love but real whores who renounced love for gain, who abandoned themselves not even out of ambition but out of indifference. The woman who is indifferent to her body and her race, that is the whore.

ODYSSEUS: Do you claim pity again?

YOUTH: Pity for such a creature is misplaced. We must be clean of the cynics to our race.

ODYSSEUS: The whores die, everyone of them. Then there is Melanthius, the traitor of all traitors. Treat him as he treated Argos but harder. Emasculate him that he may never increase his vermin kind. Remove his tongue, so he will never again speak ill of this country. Lop off the ears that always listened for slander against his country. But leave him just his eyes to see the country restored to greatness. Let him crawl in dirt for years.

YOUTH: Do you still relish dirt? You are too full of bitterness and blood. The brave may be ruthless but cruelty is alien to our race. You have learned it from another blood. It has contaminated you. Unlearn such manners now or your reign will be short and bloody and desolation will return to Ithaca.

ODYSSEUS: But traitors deserve to suffer.

YOUTH: You may decide life and death but not suffering. That is for fate and for the Gods. Our duty is to thrive, create for ourselves and destroy that which destroys us. All else is arrogant presumption and the cupidity of the low. Only the low confuse vengeance and revenge, ruthlessness and cruelty.

TELEMACHUS: Will you never leave us again?

ODYSSEUS: She did not ask questions as you do. She held the faith and believed in

me. She, a woman showed more
courage than my son. That boy
shows more courage than you. Why
did you fight today? Just to impress
someone? Is that why you fought?

TELEMACHUS: Why did I fight? Why? I... I...

YOUTH: And now who asks questions? That
is the very question you may not
ask!

ODYSSEUS: You dare tell me, the King, there is a
question that I may not ask my own
son?

YOUTH: May not ask! May never ask! Your
shadow may tell you everything and
you must listen, Odysseus.
We fought for Ithaca but my Ithaca
is not his Ithaca and his Ithaca is
never your Ithaca. Ithaca is in every
one of us the same yet not the same.
Never question us now. Never
question this burning love which
restores the world to its greatness,
this burning ineffable love which
each of us share and cannot share
is one love and yet different, the
same and not at all the same.
Rejoice that the power of darkness
has retreated for a while to its caves.
Rejoice for the light which burns
again. Rejoice Odysseus that you
have returned home a King in a

royal land again. Rejoice great King for the Homeland, the Homeland, restored after a nightmare, herself again, crying and weeping for joy, the joy of a new compact, a new union and new willingness to believe in herself. Burn and bury the shame and plant the trees again, restore and refresh the land, let the world see us proud again. Odysseus, there has been enough blood. Have you forgotten your Ithaca in your quest for knowledge? Have you forgotten why the suitors were here? Have you forgotten Ithaca? Have you forgotten your patient wife? She is waiting for Odysseus!

ODYSSEUS: I have been dreaming for years while the Homeland waited for the day that I would return. My travels across the sea were all like a long dream, a voyage of learning. And all those years she was waiting and did not complain. I was so long. I was so long! Penelope! Penelope! Ithaca! My queen! My faithful joy-in-life! I have been through madness for you and through every temptation and somehow I have survived and defeated my worst self and all my enemies.

YOUTH: Survived and a King again!

ODYSSEUS: She kept the Faith. She waited,
                  helpless and unarmed. She never
                  wavered. She waited. The beloved
                  country. My wife!

YOUTH: You have redeemed the country.

ODYSSEUS: Penelope!

*(A woman dressed entirely in white appears and rushes into
                  his arms)*

TELEMACHUS: She knew him at once.

YOUTH: The shroud has been completed.
                  Ithaca is in love again.

TELEMACHUS: Such joy. I wish to say, "Welcome to
                  my father's house" but I have
                  abused those words.
                  Oh Gods, such joy. Forgive me, I
                  cannot put into words my joy.
                  I was such a coward.

YOUTH: I do not need your words, comrade.
                  First let us dispatch the wretched
                  Melanthius with our swords and
                  spare him the suffering which only
                  a primitive darkness could relish.
                  Then we can enjoy the summer, we
                  the young. The shroud is finished,
                  the King returned.

TELEMACHUS: Homeland dear, in love, in love, you are ours again!

FINIS